For scant seconds the aircraft maintained an impossible attitude, still graceful in flight. Then the left wing tip brushed earth, and it was jerked from the sky. The aircraft cartwheeled angrily, engine screaming out of control, and exploded, orange flames mushrooming until they swallowed the entire wreckage.

They stood, frozen in unbelieving silence. Broken then by the distinctive sound of Miller's carbine in the direction of the pass, firing rapidly.

Robert Rostand

THE KILLER ELITE

ARROW BOOKS

ARROW BOOKS LTD
3 Fitzroy Square, London W1

An imprint of the Hutchinson Publishing Group

London Melbourne Sydney Auckland
Wellington Johannesburg and agencies
throughout the world

First published in
Great Britain by Hodder and Stoughton 1974
Arrow edition 1975
© Robert Rostand 1973

Made and printed in Great Britain
by The Anchor Press Ltd
Tiptree, Essex

ISBN 0 09 911130 6

AUTHOR'S NOTE

THE U.S. State Department has no Department of Security/Office of Protective Services (SYOPS). The thought that any member of the State Department might also owe allegiance to a more secretive branch of the American Government is, of course, preposterous.

Mr. John Lee, the former Labour M.P. for Reading, is very much a real person. His speech suggesting that the British Army become an elite of political assassins was given on the floor of the House of Commons in November, 1969.

PROLOGUE

LOCKEN SLID his eyes away from the four repeater screens of the infra-red warning system, each etching in thermal profile, one sector of approach to the farmhouse.

He rubbed his eyes, knowing from experience that it would do little to prevent the retina's brief retention of the images, and that already, for all practical purposes, he was night-blind. With his eyes shut he became newly aware of the all-absorbing electronic hum given off by the apparatus, and wondered, as he always did, just how long it would be before some engineer designed a machine that would take over his job completely. Not soon enough, he decided.

SYOPS had used infra-red night vision gear for more than three years now, with proven effectiveness. Locken knew in the multi-colored rendering of the surrounding English countryside he could instantly recognize the difference between a hare and a deer or, more importantly, a man—even one crawling on his stomach within 100 yards of the farmhouse. Still Locken instinctively disliked the equipment for their dulling of his own senses.

He glanced at his watch and moved his eyes back to the screens. He spoke to the man asleep on the couch a few feet away without looking at him.

"It's time, Eddie." Locken's voice was low, the tone even, a voice inclined to waste itself neither on unnecessary words nor useless inflection. He was aware that he often sounded gruff to the point of rudeness, but usually made little allowance for it. "Nearly oh-four-hundred hours. Rise and shine," he said more gently to the younger man.

"Christ!" The man on the couch sat up abruptly, blinking, wiping his eyes, then the palms of his hands on his already rumpled button-down-collar shirt. "I'll never get used to this drill."

"Milkmen do it all the time. The first ten years are the hardest."

"Somehow the thought doesn't help."

The younger man stood up, loosened his belt, and worked the holster with the heavy revolver around from the front, where it had lain heavy and ready as he slept, to his left hip, the butt facing forward.

"Have some coffee, then make the rounds," Locken said.

"Again?"

"Again," Locken responded, his voice even. "And again two hours from now. And when Perry and Crowell get here, one more time with them."

Eddie grinned at Locken. "You're a hard man, Mister."

Ten minutes later he was back, patting his broad shoulders, blowing a frosty breath in the chilled air of an early spring morning.

"Let's hear it," Locken said, looking at Eddie directly for the first time. He was a bright-faced easygoing kid, with blond hair trimmed in a bristly crew cut twenty years out of fashion. Once, reluctantly, Locken had looked at the snapshot Eddie had forced upon him. Of the equally bright-faced woman named Cheryl or Charlotte or Charlene, posing next to the framed Bronze Star earned at Danang. It was more than Locken wanted to know. For their job none of it mattered.

"All windows shuttered, locked, and wired. No seals broken. The same for the doors. Gas sensors and emergency lighting check out."

Locken nodded. "Wrodny?"

"He's asleep. Snoring like a buzz saw."

"You looked at him? You made sure it was Wrodny?" The younger man grinned sheepishly. "Go back and look, then. Make sure."

When Eddie returned he was smiling, relieved. "It's Wrodny, all right. One whiff would have been enough." He shook his head. "They all drink that much?"

Locken's eyes settled again on the repeater screens.

"Most. They're all scared. Of us. Of their own people. Some show it more than others. Most of them drink."

"Who do you suppose Wrodny is? Really, I mean."

"A member of the Czech Trade Mission. That's all we have to know."

Eddie frowned. "And what will happen to him?"

"Some people from MI5 are coming down from London with Perry and Crowell. They'll have him for the morning. Then he goes out by plane."

"After that, I meant."

"Hell, I don't know." Locken's tone was suddenly irritable. "I don't keep track. A house in Arlington until the experts find out what he brought with him. Then one more foreigner in a small town somewhere with a pension."

"Don't you ever wonder?"

For a moment Locken's eyes took on a distant squint, then snapped back and held on the younger man, without expression.

"No I don't wonder. We're not the CIA, Eddie. It's their

job to pick the brains and issue new lives. We deliver the goods, that's all. Us and Brinks. Think of SYOPS that way and you'll be a lot happier."

"I mean they're people, aren't they? With families, and feelings, just like anyone."

Locken gave Eddie a sharp look. But his voice remained even. "You don't know anything about it. Most of them are pimps or salesmen or soured idealists running scared."

"I mean, why do a job like this unless you care about people?"

"Because you're a professional. And a professional doesn't need to care. He does it for himself."

Eddie grinned at him openly. "Perry says you've never lost one." The hint of unconcealed idolatry irritated Locken.

"Perry knows better. I lost Gunter Rachman."

"Perry said Rachman hanged himself."

"Same difference." Locken jumped to his feet, as though to dismiss the topic. He stretched to his full six feet, and rolled his shoulders.

He was unnaturally slender for his height, the lean muscles and tendons showing against the large bones of his forearms. His face had none of the rounded youthfulness of the younger man's, although there were barely eight years separating them. Locken reflected he had been Eddie's age, twenty-five, when he began with SYOPS. The job, and what had happened before, showed in his face, he knew. It was as though too many years of wariness had drained away his youth prematurely, leaving his face lined and hardened before its time.

Locken picked up the Smith and Wesson automatic from the table and slipped it into the Burns-Martin holster on his belt. Without the familiar weight of it, he had reluctantly come to feel only partly dressed.

"Ready?" asked Locken.

"A bit cold around the edges," Eddie said, already slipping into the straight-backed chair in front of the bank of screens.

"Hardship breeds character," Locken said, and nearly smiled at the absurdity of it.

"And calluses," added Eddie.

"And calluses."

"I'll learn, Mike," the younger man said.

"I know," said Locken.

He watched the younger man pull the heavy revolver from his hip, a big .357 *Combat Magnum* with a four-inch barrel and custom grip. Eddie put it gently on the table. A single 158-grain bullet could split an engine block at twenty-five yards. Another item that mattered not at all. Instinctively Locken wondered how well Eddie had done on his last combat range qualification, and made a mental note to check. Even with their electronic gadgetry, if trouble came, where and how fast you put the first shot counted most.

Locken looked at his watch again. "Five minutes, Eddie. I'm going to work out the kinks. If anything jumps on the scanners, shout. Even if it's the Easter bunny."

Locken went up the stairs, his weight urging a groan from the worn fir planking.

"How about Frankenstein's monster?" Eddie said behind him.

"Him too," Locken shot back, but he was already thinking again about the farmhouse. He didn't like the feel of it.

Cap Collis himself had arranged it, and Locken admitted that strategically the farmhouse couldn't have been better. It was twenty miles from London and four miles

from Gatwick Airport, where at noon the next day
Wrodny would be put aboard an Airforce C-130. Getting
Wrodny to the farmhouse had been quick and clean.
They'd never used it as a safe house before.

It was the building itself that felt wrong. Too big, too
isolated, too many sounds of its own. The Wrodny business had broken quickly; Locken hadn't had the chance to
go over the layout as carefully as he preferred. "No
sweat," Cap Collis had told him. "Used to belong to a
mistress of Charles the First," he said, winking lewdly.
"Ought to make you happy just knowing what went on in
the place."

But about places you could never tell. Where they had
held Gunter Rachman the previous September had
checked out perfectly. An old farm with a stone-walled
longhouse, two miles from a backwater Welsh village
named Cudwyp. From a nearby pasture Rachman was to
fly via light aircraft to Shannon then aboard an Aer Lin-
gus flight to Ottawa. Locken had gone over the rough
valley nearby, first on stereo-paired aerial photographs,
then on foot. At four points they'd installed small seismic
alarms. The job had felt secure.

In the morning he had found Rachman hanging from a
light cord in the bedroom. The light cord shouldn't have
held him. It shouldn't have held anyone. When Locken
had lifted the body down he was startled at how little
Rachman weighed—less than a hundred pounds, the
pathologist said later. The oxygen content in blood sam-
ples taken from muscle tissue indicated very little struggle.
The pathologist thought Rachman must have hung there,
willing himself still, to avoid parting the slender cord
around his neck. What made him change his mind about
defecting no one could guess. You couldn't tell about people, either.

Locken stopped outside Wrodny's door and listened a moment to the old man's rumbling snore. He opened the door quickly, automatic in hand. Then he shut it and moved off along the hall slowly, listening.

At the end of the hall was a white-tiled bathroom with all the warmth, to Locken's mind, of a public urinal. He knew from experience at that hour of the morning his blood sugar was at its lowest. His reflexes became dull and velvety. Sleep tried to crawl into his brain, and on the job Locken never slept.

He bent to the tap, took a mouthful of cold water and swallowed a five-grain, heart-shaped Benzedrine. He pulled the heavy automatic again from the holster and balanced it carefully on the edge of the washbasin, within arm's reach of the shower. He stripped off his clothing quickly. The drug, combined with his ritual cold douse, would put him on edge long past relief at 0800 hours.

He turned on the cold tap and stepped beneath the icy stream of water. The biting shock made him gasp. He took a deep breath and for several minutes let the stinging jet of water play over his taut trapezius muscles then up and down along his spine. His hand was already reaching to turn off the cold tap when he heard the toilet flush.

The anger at Eddie for leaving the scanners rose in him uncontrollably. In other businesses inexperience might serve as an excuse. In their business there were no excuses.

He flung back the shower curtain, the sharp words catching in his throat.

Within the milliseconds it took his brain to search his memory of the vast picture file kept by SYOPS of agents, friendly or otherwise, Locken knew with certainty that he had never seen the man standing in the doorway before.

High forehead, sloping back slightly to dark, wavy hair. A face no older or younger than his own, already warped

into a good-natured grin. The grin was belied in its friend-
liness only by the heavy Mauser pistol in the man's right
hand, the yawning gape of its silencer aimed at Locken's
chest.

"Dead," the man said. "They're both dead." Locken
knew with sickening certainty it was true. "The young one
was slow." The man shook his head sadly and even as he
did so the first shot seemed to split Locken's left leg in
half.

The impact of the bullet drove him back against the
white-tiled shower wall, his shattered knee collapsing beneath him. In a flailing, instinctive movement he shifted
his weight arching his back, pushing himself toward the
pistol balanced precariously on the edge of the washbasin
scant feet away. If only his movements were not slow
motion, movements in a dream, barely acknowledged by
the man who moved a step toward him and sighted carefully, the round ugly mouth of the silencer gaping at the
end of the pistol held at arm's length.

To Locken it seemed as though the second bullet tore
away his outstretched right arm, spinning him helplessly
into a heap at the bottom of the tub. His eyes fought to
focus, the pain from the extremities of his body converg-
ing on his heart, then spreading upward and outward until
his entire being cried out and the cry finally escaped his
lips as a hoarse gurgle.

Above him Locken saw the passionless eyes below the
high forehead, examining as carefully as a doctor might a
patient on an operating table.

The one thought in Locken's mind, clung to desperately
like a single bit of flotsam in a sea of emptiness, was that
he was still alive, and he shouldn't have been.

The man slowly, methodically, unscrewed the energy-
robbing silencer from the barrel of the Mauser. Then he

reached across with his left hand and turned off the shower.

"I'm Hansen," he said, raising the pistol. "I thought you might like to know." It was almost an apology.

Then he bent forward toward Locken, pointing the pistol down at the tightened knot of genitalia and pubic hair already constricted by shock. He hesitated an instant then squeezed the trigger.

"THREE," repeated Alec Ashton-Smyth gravely, "all into England within the past twenty-four hours."

He leaned back and glanced away from the other two men at the table.

The table was his favorite, in the northeast corner of St. James's second floor dining room, isolated enough to ensure their conversation would remain unobtrusively private.

Ashton-Smyth knew that sitting as he was, with his head turned just so, his bold profile was etched against the buildings along Piccadilly framed in the high window at his back, and bathed at that moment in rare autumn sunlight. The pose shifted attention from his gaunt, pocked cheeks, and he had been told by his P.A. that it gave the impression of great strength. Ashton-Smyth visualized his appearance at that moment as one of profound concern over the matter he had immediately introduced into the discussion, after they had ordered lunch.

He was in fact deciding between the club's excellent Montilla, and a bottle from the dwindling stock of Leoville Poyferré '59. Pressed, he would have settled for either. He had arrived in much too great a hurry for his customary stop at the bar.

To his left he heard Wilton mutter a "good heavens." "I

mean, if they are here . . ." He sat back staring at Ashton-Smyth apprehensively, chewing at the ends of his large walrus moustache.

Wilton had the added niggling habit of letting the ends of his sentences dangle. Opinion in Ashton-Smyth's department was that it probably went for his thoughts as well. He had liaisoned with the Foreign Office through Willy before. This time he thanked himself for his luck in the draw.

"All right, Alec," said the third man at the table. "Let's cut the crap."

Ashton-Smyth sighed and shifted his gaze reluctantly to Cap Collis.

Nearly everything about Collis went against his grain. His manner of dressing, which despite the efforts of a reputable bespoke tailor, still managed to achieve the slick, seedy look of a commercial traveler. But most of all the accent—that broad, brassy American accent which seemed to Ashton-Smyth the exaggerated caricature of a nightclub mimic.

It disturbed Ashton-Smyth no end that he needed Cap Collis desperately.

Collis put both hands on the table and leaned toward him. "Who are they? And why are they here?"

"Most disturbing, Alec, really," said Wilton. His voice drifted off.

Ashton-Smyth tried to catch the eye of old Stokes, the wine steward. Failing, he sighed again almost imperceptibly and removed the three salmon-colored memos his P.A. had hastily assembled that morning, from his inside jacket pocket.

He cleared his throat, which felt terribly dry. "A man we know as Étienne Bouche landed at Heathrow yesterday afternoon, a SABENA flight from Brussels. Forged Belgian passport of good quality, apparently. No customs declaration. He whisked through without notice."

Cap Collis waved a hand at the memo. "I don't care about that crap, Alec. Who is this Étienne Bouche?" He pronounced Étienne, *eighteen*.

Ashton-Smyth found Collis's manner more abrasive than usual. He spoke, nonetheless, in an even tone he knew revealed nothing of his own feelings about the matter at hand. He was in fact quite upset, for reasons that he hoped would remain entirely private.

Ashton-Smyth answered Collis directly. "A former Colonel in the French Army, a *pied noir* born in Algiers. During the Algerian war he belonged to the Red Hand, a violent forerunner of the Secret Army. Supported the General's putsch, naturally, and was later accused of attempting to assassinate de Gaulle." He allowed himself a thin smile. "But then wasn't everyone? Bouche was definitely responsible for the murder of a German arms dealer selling weapons to the Algerian F.L.N. in August 1957. Blew him through the roof of his Mercedes in front of the Libyan Embassy in Bonn."

"Good grief," moaned Wilton predictably.

Ashton-Smyth ignored him. "After the Algerian business, Bouche began selling his talents on the open market." He lowered his voice. "There is even talk that Bouche was involved in the Mondlane affair. A gelignite-filled chair the instrument of death, I believe. It seems Bouche is quite expert with explosives."

He slipped a small snapshot from a large leather billfold and handed it past Wilton to Cap Collis. "Six years old, I'm afraid."

Cap Collis studied it with an intensity that surprised Ashton-Smyth. "Looks like a preacher."

"Yes, he is rather pious-faced," agreed Ashton-Smyth, distracted. He had at last caught the eye of old Stokes. He damned himself again for not taking the precaution of a drink or two before lunch. Invariably it settled his nerves.

Collis shoved the photo back toward Ashton-Smyth. "All right, Bouche is one."

Ashton-Smyth shuffled the memos, put them flat on the table, and folded his hands in his lap as he read. His hands often trembled in the morning. "The second is a Cuban named Roqué. Entered England in similar manner. Forged passport, no customs declaration. Arrived last night through Manchester aboard an Iberia flight from Madrid. Nothing much in our records, I'm afraid, except that Roqué was with Castro . . ."

Cap Collis interrupted him with a curt wave of his hand. "I know about Roqué. With Castro all right. In the Sierra Maestra and the whole distance after that. One of the few."

"We heard Roqué was involved in some trouble," Ashton-Smyth probed casually, "in Miami."

Collis pulled his chin and smiled at Ashton-Smyth. "Now, Alec, you know exactly what happened in Miami— Miami Beach, to be finickity about it. A shooting, about five years back, in the lobby of the Fontainebleau Hotel. Roqué shot down a couple of characters who used to work for Rolando Masferrer, Havana's police chief under Batista. Drilled them both through a newspaper then walked out the front door, directed a cop toward the sound of the shooting, and caught a cab, as cool as you will."

"Yes," said Ashton-Smyth mildly, "but we lost track after that."

"Well now," said Cap Collis. "Roqué later appeared—I said appeared—to fall out with Castro. Left Cuba about the time Che dropped out of the picture. Some say they went together."

"What a vile-sounding fellow," said Wilton, his jaw drooping slightly.

"Woman," said Ashton-Smyth. "Elise Roqué."

Beneath his moustache Wilton's mouth became a small dark *oh*.

Collis looked straight at Ashton-Smyth. "Who's number three?"

Ashton-Smyth met Collis's gaze levelly. "Rickard Hansen."

When Stokes arrived, Ashton-Smyth ordered wine and turned to Cap Collis.

"You will have claret, won't you, Collis?"

The other man didn't appear to hear him. Collis's face had hardened around a mouth open slightly in thought. Ashton-Smyth dismissed Stokes with a nod, pleased with himself at the dramatically precise timing of his delivery. He took great satisfaction in even small victories.

"So he's back in England," Collis breathed finally.

"I thought you might be interested."

"I'm more than that. Yes, I am."

"Wasn't he the one . . ." Wilton began, raising a questioning finger.

Collis nodded. "Wrodny. Seven months ago he got to Wrodny and two of my boys. Killed one and ruined the other. My best."

"For whom?" asked Wilton, wide-eyed.

Collis's eyes darted between Wilton and Ashton-Smyth. "Well now, we're just not sure. The Russkies maybe. Or the Czechs. Or the SDECE*. A lot of people would have been happy to see Wrodny's mouth shut. It might have been you, for all I know."

"Really, Collis," said Ashton-Smyth, letting his mouth turn down in distaste.

* Service de Documentation Extérieure et Contre-Espionage: France's counter-intelligence service.

"Hansen works for whoever signs the check." Collis slapped his thighs. "Which makes everything just dandy. I got the Vice President blowing through here tomorrow, and lurking out there somewhere"—he gestured broadly at the high window behind Ashton-Smyth—"are three cool-headed professional killers."

Ashton-Smyth thought it all a bit overdone. "I humbly suggest the august gentleman might sleep soundly nonetheless."

"You can't be sure, Alec, and I don't want you to get smart about that. Just mention assassin to a government security man these days, or any politician for that matter, and he'll pee green."

"Those three couldn't care less about your Vice President," Ashton-Smyth said, pausing an instant to emphasize what followed. "They are here to assassinate Moses Nyoka."

Wilton's face went crimson. Ashton-Smyth prayed he wouldn't become emotional.

"Moses Nyoka?" Collis repeated.

"Come now, Collis, you've heard of the man."

"Hell yes," said Collis irritably. "He was tossed out of Buwanda three, maybe four years ago."

"Not exactly tossed out. A palace coup while he was in England. Visit to his schoolgirl daughter, I believe. The usual shopping spree."

"That's unfair, Alec," said Wilton. "It was a state visit . . ."

"Same difference," said Collis. "I don't see why this new guy . . ."

"General Aman," prompted Ashton-Smyth. "Houari Aman. Nyoka's brother-in-law, and a Muslim to boot."

"Why Aman would want Nyoka taken care of at this late date . . ."

"I thought your morning intelligence summary might have given you a clue." Ashton-Smyth's voice was heavy with irony.

Cap Collis grinned. "Now, Alec, you know SYOPS is at the tail end of the routing slip. Besides, I can't face that crap before lunch."

"At this moment Aman is struggling with the first organized attempt to push him from power."

Wilton confirmed it with a nod.

"Another coup?" asked Collis.

"Hardly," replied Ashton-Smyth. "Aman has the civil guard in his pocket. This is a full-fledged uprising. Students, the labor unions, the Western tribes, naturally, and of course the urban riff-raff. Fighting broke out late yesterday."

"Caught us all napping, I'm afraid," Wilton said.

Ashton-Smyth eyed Wilton silently and went on. "The final edition of the *Times* picked it up this morning. By this afternoon it will be headlines. Oh, yes, the dissidents have a slogan." Ashton-Smyth gave Collis an arch grin. "Nyoka returns."

"That's nice," nodded Collis. "Simple to grab." The easygoing manner slid away. "That still don't add up to a try at assassinating Moses Nyoka."

"Don't be absurd."

It was Wilton who made the pronouncement with a firm authority that brought Collis's head around. Wilton's face had taken on extraordinary life. His puckish mouth worked feverishly at the drooping ends of his moustache. Below it a small plump hand fingered the soiled knot of his club tie handed carelessly at the collar of a tired white shirt.

Ashton-Smyth remembered the photograph he had once seen of Wilton, as a rather robust R.A.F. Wing Commander. The only recognizable similarity with the Wilton he had come to know, that same dashing moustache. But Willy wasn't dashing. He was a round, gray, frustrated man whose war record had earned him a comfortable sinecure in Whitehall's East African section. Without the necessary charm or proper connections there he had languished. He was knowledgeable, everyone said so, but he was also without power of any kind. For once Ashton-Smyth looked upon it as a virtue. Willy's impotence would keep him safe from the establishment's wrath for involving Collis in what should have remained an internal matter. Ashton-Smyth would have been reluctant to explain his motives.

"If Nyoka returns to Buwanda," Wilton was saying confidently, "Aman will go over like a ninepin."

Collis leaned toward Wilton. "What makes you think so?"

Wilton blinked, flushed, patted his moustache with a napkin. "Tell me, Captain. Have you ever seen him?"

Ashton-Smyth saw Collis wince. Wilton had committed the unpardonable error of calling Cap Collis "Captain." For God only knew what reason, Cap was his given name, not an abbreviation of military rank. As far as Ashton-Smyth knew, Collis had never been military. A lawyer in some small Florida town before becoming European head of SYOPS. Ashton-Smyth had always wondered how he managed the jump. At that instant he could have throttled Willy. He had seen less sensitive negotiations founder on smaller blunders.

"Now I can't say I have," said Cap Collis. "But to tell it true, all them African politicos look the same to me. Like Chinese."

Wilton scarcely heard him. "Born leader, Nyoka. Tremendous figure of a man. Six feet three or four and must

weigh twenty stone. Almost seventy now, but God, still a
man. Pulled Buwanda into a country when East Africa
came apart, and gave it the kind of pride in itself old Jomo
gave Kenya. Nyoka still has the country in the palm of his
hand."

"I believe Willy knew him at university, Collis." Ashton-
Smyth suddenly felt protective of Wilton. He had seen Cap
Collis's bad temper at work before.

Willy looked away blankly. "Cracker fast bowler for
Balliol he was. Have a picture of him in a test against
Christ's I'll never forget. There was young Moses Nyoka
approaching the wicket like some graceful animal across
the steppes, decked out in brilliant whites, of course. I was
sure I was watching something of a miracle."

"Cricket's a miracle all right," said Cap Collis. He was
watching Wilton, but his attention seemed elsewhere.

"Tribal scars, an ear maimed by some childhood acci-
dent in the bush, but dressed like a civilized man, by God,
and as proud and powerful as a man could be, white or
black. It was as though, right there, I was watching the
generation that jumped a thousand years of history. I
knew something spectacular would become of Nyoka, and
I was right. Ashton-Smyth shifted his teaspoon against a
salad fork, the sound bringing Wilton's gaze back to the
table. "I was right," he repeated, and looked limply
around, as though the effort of sustained thought had totally drained him.

"Well now," said Cap Collis, nodding. "I guess this
Aman has a good reason for wanting Nyoka to stay
away." He smiled pleasantly. Then the smile narrowed.
"I'm still not convinced those three are here to kill him."

"I am," Ashton-Smyth said firmly.

His EYES searched nervously for the familiar bent gait of old Stokes. An odd, unreasonable panic tugged at Ashton-Smyth's stomach when he realized, that with the Parliament crowd swelling the bar and dining room, Stokes might be some minutes. He badly needed a drink. He forced himself to look again at Cap Collis, who sat none too patiently waiting for him to explain.

"Tell me, Collis," he said, with labored evenness, "have you ever heard of John Lee?"

"Sounds like a lot of people I've heard of."

"Member of Parliament here a few years back. Absolute terror on military spending. Made a brilliant speech in the Commons in sixty-nine with a radical proposal on how to cut the size of the British Army. Lee's idea was to turn it into a small elite of political assassins."

"Bit of a crank," said Wilton.

Ashton-Smyth looked at Willie with open coolness. "His logic was that a small power like Britain couldn't hope to compete militarily with the superpowers. Lee thought in this day the political assassin was more fearsome than the Bomb, hence a better tool of diplomacy. His speech made quite a splash in the dailies."

"Smart man," said Collis without inflection. "What's the connection with Aman?"

"Aman caught wind of Lee's idea and fancied it. Less than a month after Lee's speech he abolished Buwanda's army with great fanfare, saying that a poor country couldn't afford such luxuries—Lee's words quote and unquote. Of course Aman still has the police and a civil guard of 1500 crack troops."

"And a fat Swiss bank account by now, I bet," Collis said. "What's the point?"

"I haven't had a chance to make it yet," snapped Ashton-Smyth peevishly.

He carefully rearranged the teaspoon and salad fork a second time. "Aman then proceeded to procure two dozen of the best professional killers he could find. He supports them very lavishly in an estate outside the capital. He has let the word leak out that if anyone conspires against him, who knows what might happen to them. We suspect Bouche, Roqué, and Hansen are now employed by Aman."

Collis studied Ashton-Smyth, then nodded thoughtfully. "He picked himself some good ones."

"But I'm afraid he didn't, don't you see?"

Collis moved forward slightly. "No, I don't see."

"Last night we received a phone call," Ashton-Smyth went on hurriedly, "to the correct number, I might add. A man speaking English, with an accent, of course. Described the whole business."

"What do you mean, the whole business?" Collis's tone became harsh.

"Mentioned Bouche, Roqué, and Hansen, the fictitious names they were traveling under, and their flight numbers. We verified it later, of course. Then he told us they would kill Nyoka when and where they could. Without Nyoka, the revolt against Aman will collapse like a house of cards."

"Information in exchange for what?"

"Nothing."

Collis shuffled in his chair uneasily. "It doesn't wash, Alex. Those three are pros. Which means careful. And they're moving fast. No one would have found out that kind of information, not that quick, anyway. If they had, it would have cost you plenty."

"That's the conclusion we came to," said Ashton-Smyth. "Only one answer to it."

"Is that right."

"The caller is one of them."

"Heavens," said Wilton.

Ashton-Smyth's wintry stare held on Collis. "One of those three is trying to make very sure Moses Nyoka remains alive."

Cap Collis leaned forward, his voice taking on a brittle edge.

"So why are we sitting here sweating the arrival of a bottle of claret?"

Ashton-Smyth ignored the implication. "I can't risk the chance Nyoka might be killed."

Cap Collis grunted impatiently. "What's he doing sitting home waiting by the fire? He ought to be in Buwanda."

"As of one hour ago Nyoka appeared blissfully ignorant of events in Buwanda. I'm sure he knows nothing of the assassins. My guess is Aman caught wind of the revolt and forced it off ahead of schedule." Ashton-Smyth shrugged slightly. "Whatever happened, Nyoka's people failed to alert him in time. God knows how they managed to buy out one of those gunmen."

"Funny thing about money," Cap Collis said in a monotone.

Ashton-Smyth continued: "Exactly what Nyoka will do when he learns of the revolt is the big question. I have men watching his flat right now. We think he'll try to get to Buwanda as quickly as he can."

Cap Collis shook his head. "That ain't the big question, Alec. The big question is what do you want from me?"

Ashton-Smyth spoke the words as lightly as he dared. "I'd like you to see Nyoka safely out of Britain."

"SYOPS?" Collis laughed sharply. "You're kidding."

Ashton-Smyth leaned toward him. "Let me be perfectly frank with you, Collis."

"Uh-huh."

"If Nyoka returns to power in Buwanda we run the risk of having Anglo-Buwanda Copper, the entire Lonwan Syndicate, plus a number of other British enterprises expelled, just as they were after independence."

"My, my," said Cap Collis. "I wouldn't have thought you could afford that."

"No, we cannot," Ashton-Smyth said firmly. "Aman is a more . . . reasonable man. Unless we appear too helpful to Moses Nyoka. Then he could be equally unpleasant."

"You mean he might toss you out himself. Get some other friendly power to help run the copper industry." Cap Collis squinted thoughtfully. "I bet Kennecott or Anaconda would be delighted."

"He might," Ashton-Smyth replied coolly, "ask the Russians."

Collis tilted his head to one side. "Now, Alec, that just ain't the stomach-twister it used to be. You ought to worry more about what happens if Nyoka rides back into power."

Ashton-Smyth rolled his eyes upward, putting his hands palm to palm. "We're praying that won't happen. Aman's civil guard, thankfully, is first-rate."

"British-trained officers, no doubt."

Ashton-Smyth let the comment pass. "Without Nyoka's

presence to elevate their cause I wouldn't think the rebels stand a chance."

Cap Collis's eyes rested directly on Ashton-Smyth. "Then why don't you let nature take its course?"

Wilton stirred to attention, then sat up straight. "You mean let the assassins . . ." He frowned at Collis, his chin jutting forward in a poor caricature of an angry Churchill. "Unthinkable."

"Oh, I don't know," said Cap Collis, looking at Ashton-Smyth.

Ashton-Smyth averted Collis's gaze, his eyes stabbing the room for the sight of Stokes. He made a mental note to talk with the Secretary about that man. He sighed. "Actually we did give some thought to killing Nyoka, ourselves." He looked up to see if Collis's face showed any surprise. There was none. "Off the record, we couldn't care less what happens to Nyoka. We gave him asylum three years ago to soothe relations with a number of African states. We'd rather have buried him." Wilton started to protest, but Ashton-Smyth cut him off with an icy stare. He leaned toward Collis. "But if he were assassinated on British soil there would be the devil to pay."

"It might be worth it," said Collis, smiling.

"It would not," said Ashton-Smyth, becoming agitated. "The diplomatic uproar would be frightful, and Buwanda isn't the only place we have economic interests. I have no need to tell you we'd be tied to Nyoka's death one way or the other. You could bet the Chinese would whisper it throughout Africa, and probably your own CIA as well."

"I wouldn't be surprised, Alec," Collis said. "I wouldn't be surprised at all."

"Conspiracy has such a nasty sound these days, and I'm told by the experts it translates rather easily."

"Then do yourself a favor," said Collis, "and throw

Nyoka into protective custody until this blows over. For his own good, naturally."

Collis sat back then, the barest hint of a smile on his unmistakably American face. Ashton-Smyth had the distinct impression Collis actually enjoyed seeing him squirm. The sure knowledge that his time would come sustained Ashton-Smyth at moments like this.

He took a firm hold on his waning patience and forced himself to return the smile with a knowing grin of his own.

"I'm afraid diplomacy is no longer that simple, Collis. We wouldn't fool a soul. If Nyoka wants to try to reach Buwanda we can do nothing to stop him." He held up a long index finger dramatically. "Put one friendly hand on Nyoka's shoulder and we'll have the O.A.U. plus the U.N. Security Council screaming interference in African affairs, or some other such rubbish."

"Them being exactly right doesn't help much, either." Collis's voice was agreeably pleasant.

Ashton-Smyth shook his head and immediately wished he hadn't. He felt almost faint. "Where Nyoka is concerned we're damned if we do or don't. We find it absolutely imperative to avoid making any gesture toward him which could be interpreted as taking sides." He looked meaningfully at Wilton. "Isn't that right, Willy?"

Wilton bobbed his head in ready agreement. "Absolutely, Alec."

Cap Collis smiled at the two of them. "Now you've been totally frank with me, how about telling me the truth?"

Ashton-Smyth's pocked cheeks hollowed slightly. "Whatever do you mean?"

"I mean that political double-talk may be so. But it's not the only reason you want me to chauffeur Nyoka out of Britain for you." He made a deprecating wave of his hand.

"Pshaw, you could find a dozen old cronies from the S.O.E. just itching to strap on an operation again, discreetly of course."

Ashton-Smyth snatched a Benson & Hedges from his cigarette case, lit it quickly, and sucked the smoke deeply into his lungs. He was amused at how well Collis's open, country-boy manner concealed an intuitively suspicious mind.

"The truth is," Ashton-Smyth said slowly, "Nyoka won't give our people the time of day. Convincing him to trust us with his life is an absolute impossibility." Ashton-Smyth dragged again on the cigarette and let the smoke out through his nose. "You see, Nyoka discovered he was on our blacklist."

Cap Collis raised his eyebrows in astonishment. "Blacklist?"

Ashton-Smyth eyed his mock-surprise with amusement. "Come now, Collis. We all deny such lists exist, yet we all have them. Your intelligence agencies would scarcely function without their lists. Every department of every government in the world has a 'blacklist,' even if it stops with their own employees. Those to whom no aid would be offered even if they were drowning. People to eliminate, governments to withhold aid from, politicians to ignore; because they lack the proper humility, kindred spirit, or ideology."

"What an interesting idea," said Collis.

"Nyoka was on ours. Any effort we make to help him would be suspect immediately. He is a very cunning and difficult old man."

"So you want me to do your chores for you?"

"The less this reeks of something official or British, the better."

"And what if I don't buy it?"

Ashton-Smyth paused. He played his trump card delicately. "I think you owe me a favor."

Cap Collis chuckled. "I've been waiting for that."

Ashton-Smyth lowered his voice. "It was not easy to pass off the Wrodny business as suicide. Not with two bullets in the back of his head." Ashton-Smyth glanced at Wilton. "Best forget you heard that, Willy."

Wilton blinked. "Sorry, Alec. . . . What?"

Cap Collis smiled. "I appreciated it, Alec, you know I did. But SYOPS can't touch this officially for the same reasons you can't. The State Department of the government of the United States, of which we are but one small, underbudgeted office, cannot stick its fingers into another country's internal affairs. Now you know that, Alec."

There was an uneasy silence, until Cap Collis grinned, reached around behind his head with his left hand, and tugged at his right earlobe.

"But I just might be able to help. Unofficially."

The relief showed visibly on Ashton-Smyth's face. "I would appreciate it greatly, Collis."

"Yes, sir. I just might know somebody who would find this a very interesting proposition."

Beyond Cap Collis, Ashton-Smyth saw Stokes emerge through an archway and move toward them. A dark, slope-shouldered bottle balanced in the direct center of a silver tray carried with unfailing steadiness. If only lunch were tasty, it seemed to Ashton-Smyth, the day might turn out quite well.

In the taxi moving swiftly along Kensington Road toward Holland Park, Cap Collis hummed cheerfully at the back of the driver's head beyond the glass partition.

The hour since he had left St. James's had crackled with

the kind of activity that provided Cap Collis one of his few unalloyed pleasures in life. He knew he was one of those rare individuals fortunate enough to enjoy organization for its own sake. He had been blessed with an even rarer ability to move decisively without remorse over what might result; it was a quality of great generals. In his mind, the separate elements had fitted together with almost unnerving smoothness. At moments like this Cap Collis entertained the thought, revealed only by an unguarded grin, that somewhere there might be a God after all.

At a traffic light the taxi stopped next to a metallic blue Alvis Coupe. A very pretty girl glared up at the traffic light from behind the wheel. She glanced at Cap Collis, who smiled and nodded through the taxi window. "Better to be born lucky than rich, ain't it, lady?"

The girl turned her head sharply with faint distaste; the Alvis leapt forward with the change of the light. "And don't you know it," said Cap Collis, watching the blue car speed away in the distance.

Then he sat back, the smile gone, and rode the rest of the way in silence.

3

FROM THE second-floor landing Locken could hear the stereo playing inside his flat, one flight up.

The record was an old Mose Allison L.P. that Liz couldn't stand. For her it would have been the Stones, or Joplin, or if she was low, the Swingle Singers mangling Bach.

Steps. One long flight, seemingly longer than the other two flights combined, although in actuality two steps less than either. Exactly twenty-three steps he knew better than a postman knows his route. Until a few months before, he had never thought of steps one way or the other. Steps as enemies or steps as friends, depending on their arrangement, height, and number. Locken leaned on the banister, letting his left arm do the work. Two months before, he had needed a cane and plenty of time. Improvement will come in short steps, the surgeon had told him. Locken hadn't appreciated the full irony of his remark.

He walked into his apartment knowing exactly who would be there and precisely where he would be sitting.

Cap Collis sprawled in the single overstuffed armchair, his heels resting on the edge of the warped oak table in the center of the room. Liz had found the table in a junk furniture store in South London and had finally convinced

Locken that the warp was the essential part of its character. An open bottle of Beam's Choice rested on the table
within arm's reach of Cap Collis.

In the corner Liz was curled on the cane-backed couch,
her face in a *Mademoiselle*, her eyes unmoving. Her usually gentle mouth was pinched tightly, signifying to
Locken her own particular brand of quiet fury.

"That's a nice tune," said Cap Collis, greeting Locken
with a raised glass. "Saw him sing it once in a dive on
Capitol Hill. The record's better."

Locken shut the door behind him, threw his topcoat
onto the table and moved around it, aware that Cap Collis's eyes followed his every step.

Liz blinked a warm unspoken "hello."

Locken's eyes moved to Collis. "It must be the second
of February. Hello, Cap. You see your shadow?"

"Sharp a wit as ever," said Cap Collis, smiling. "How
about the rest of you?"

"The little old lady I handled today never knew what
hit her." Locken turned down the stereo. "Coffee, Liz? Do
you mind?"

"She's been keeping me fine company," said Collis.

"I definitely do not mind," said Liz, rising. She rolled
her eyes behind Collis's back and gave Locken a con-
spirator's grin.

Collis's eyes rested on the curve of her hips the distance
to the kitchen. Then he turned and looked at Locken
curiously over the top of his whiskey.

"Wouldn't have thought you had much to offer these
days."

"What's on your mind, Cap?" He made no effort to
conceal his impatience or explain. Cap Collis had been out
of his life for almost six months, from the day Locken had
walked unsteadily out of the second-floor office in an

Edwardian town house near Grosvenor Square which
served as SYOPS' European headquarters. A Standard
Form 50, folded neatly in his pocket, had been the official
end of eight years of his life, and any allegiance he might
have had to Cap Collis. Locken knew him well enough to
feel no guilt whatsoever in his total lack of affection for
the man.

Cap Collis cackled dryly. "On my mind? Merely a polite
inquiry about your health."

"You tell me."

"Well now . . ." Collis prodded his neck with an index
finger. "I know you just spent a not too pleasant hour with
a very classy Chinese gal named Miss Heather Lee, who
also happens to have a couple of degrees in physical ther-
apy from McGill. And before that, you and an ex-Royal
Sergeant Major named Dulaney had a forty-minute tête-à
tête in a very classy gym in South Kensington. The story
goes you think the two of them can put you back together."

"What else?" said Locken, only partly surprised at the
depth of Collis's snooping.

"I know a certain orthopedic surgeon who says, given a
year or so, they stand a pretty good chance. With the
body, that is. But right now you got fifteen degrees of
movement in your right elbow, and nine ounces of alumi-
num and Teflon making up for a shattered left patella.
You ain't doing many chin-ups these days, Mike. Without
a knee brace that left leg of yours is nothing but a wet
noodle."

"For the record Cap, I'm equipped well enough for the
future I have in mind."

"I sincerely hope so, Mike."

"I'm a retired gentleman with a fat disability pension.
I'm on the verge of becoming a human being again. Don't
spoil it."

"Oh, I believe you. That girl looks mighty comforting, whatever is or ain't going on between you." He made an expansive sweep of the room with one hand. "You got yourself a cozy little place." Collis's face rounded with a grin. "Bet you even found yourself a hobby."

Collis knew the absurdity of it as well as he did. He neither skied, boated, nor played tennis. He was without club memberships, and had never knowingly ventured into a garden. Golf and chess were too drawn out and niggling. Bridge was unthinkable, as were prolonged associations with the people who played it. He lacked enough money to gamble properly, although the test of self-discipline necessary to win, another time, might have appealed to him. Once there had been a passion; the wrong thing, the wrong place. Later there had only been his skill. Now, none of that.

Collis's eyes were still on him. "Yes, sir. What more could a man want?"

Locken stood up quickly and went into the kitchen. "Forget the coffee." He took a glass from the cupboard, walked back to the living room and poured himself a shot from the bottle of whiskey. "As a man I worked for used to say, 'Let's cut the crap.'"

Collis stood up, walked to the rolltop desk in the corner, and placed the telephone on top of it into a drawer.

"They got a gizmo now can tap right through the line, on or off the hook."

"Out with it, Cap."

Collis leaned toward him. "How would you like a crack at Rickard Hansen?"

Locken felt the involuntary spasm tighten the pit of his stomach. For a brief instant there was the vivid remembrance of pain, a flash of the high forehead, the careful eyes looking down at him. Locken wondered how much

longer the mere mention of a man's name would affect
him in that way. He had used SYOPS sources to find out
all there was to know about Hansen; the facts hadn't
helped at all.

A South African, born in Durban, raised in Tanganyika
before it became Tanzania. At twenty Hansen was already
one of the top professional hunters in East Africa, and by
twenty-two had blown it, killing animals driven purposely
from the game reserves, a lost license, the revengeful murder of a game ranger. Two years later he fought with
Moise Tshombe's crack army of white mercenaries during
Katanga's unsuccessful war of secession from the Congo.
Les Affreux, the Africans called them. The frightful ones.
And for good reason. Next, a brief tour as bodyguard to
an unpopular sheik in one of the Trucial States, followed
by the big time. The assassination of a wealthy Jew in
Beirut; the murder of a union official in Cleveland; a contract with the IRA provisionals eliminating British army
officers at one thousand pounds per head. Then Wrodny.

Hansen worked with equal allegiance to whoever paid
him. But Locken guessed that money was the smallest part
of it. Hansen liked the tough ones. He enjoyed the game,
and he had never been beaten.

The night Wrodny died, Locken thought he knew how
Hansen breached their security. Why he chose later to
cripple instead of kill was a question that never left Lock-
en's mind.

He sensed the look on his face answered Cap Collis's
question in the clearest possible way.

"He's back in England," said Collis. "Him and two others. Here to terminate some African honcho name of
Nyoka."

"Former Prime Minister of Buwanda."

"And hoping to be future Prime Minister of Buwanda,"

said Collis. "I just came from a boozy lunch at St. James's with a guy I know from MI5, with one of those hyphenated names. We'll call him Smith, which is close enough. Brought along some boob from Whitehall called Willy something-or-other. Seems they have themselves a little problem." Cap Collis explained about the revolt in Buwanda and Aman sending the assassination team to kill Moses Nyoka. "Old Hyphen Smith figures Nyoka's going to make a break for Buwanda. Spent half lunch persuading me to help keep him alive and the other half filling my wine glass in thanks."

"But why ask you instead of using his own people?"

In a way it was a compliment. Everyone knew the CIA had brazenly infiltrated the State Department. SYOPS had managed to keep itself clean. As Collis had said, in the jargon Locken despised, it was an absolute necessity if SYOPS was to remain credible.

Collis grunted. "A hatful of political reasons that don't add up to as much as a couple of other things. Nyoka's a crafty old beggar, evidently, and caught wind that the British have had it in for him a long time. He wouldn't trust Hyphen Smith's people with his lunch money. There's another reason." Cap Collis gave what Locken knew was his cynical smile.

"I couldn't guess."

"You could if you tried. Hyphen Smith is looking around for somebody to blame. Personally he's scared stiff. He cares more about his job than any smear on the government. And he has a hunch those three stand a good chance of getting to Nyoka. Hell, Kennedy said the most dangerous thing in the world to a politico is a man with a rifle. If Nyoka gets it, Hyphen Smith doesn't want to be remembered as the man in charge of his security. He'd rather be able to point a finger." Cap Collis grinned broadly. "First principle of government: If things can go wrong, have someone handy to blame. They're still blaming Herbert Hoover for the Depression."

Locken looked at him narrowly. "And you bought a piece of it."

"Unofficially. With Hansen involved I'd have taken the job with no favors asked, and that's a fact."

"Who's in it besides Hansen?"

"A mad bomber named Bouche." A smile spread across Collis's face. "And Elise Roqué."

"Elise."

"I thought you'd like that. Going to be just like old home week."

Behind him, Locken was aware that Liz had entered the room. He wondered how much she had heard. Very little, quite probably, for Collis's reaction had been almost immediate. His quick glance sidewise followed by the deliberate stroll to the table. A whiskey poured slowly and stared into. Cap's silence in such circumstances, Locken remembered, could have the quality of a burning fuse.

"Okay," Liz said. "A girl can tell when she's not wanted." The lightness in her voice was strained. Locken looked around, but her eyes were already moving away. "I'm late for work, Mike. I have to go."

She slid off toward the bedroom, the door clicking shut behind her.

"Nice," said Collis, raising his eyebrows. "Where does a lady like that work this time of day?"

"Rehearsal, a club in Mayfair. She sings." His answer had been mechanical. The name Elise Roqué had wedged itself into his thoughts.

"You must be one helluva good talker," observed Collis, twisting an extra meaning from the words.

"Stick to business," said Locken sharply.

"This is business. You know what I think about women."

"I'm not sure I do."

Cap's grin was ugly. "Ought to be blind, deaf, and kept flat on their backs. She know anything about you?"

"Enough."

"About your work, Mike. I don't give a damn about your anatomy."

"Only what she's guessed. More, probably, than I'd want her to."

Collis thought for a moment then dismissed it with a jump of his shoulders. "Of course I haven't told you the best part yet."

"You always do save the best for last."

"One of them three is a ring-in. For some reason I can't figure, he'd be perfectly happy to see his two buddies blow it and Nyoka go home without a scratch."

"You said *he*." Locken leaned toward him. "What do you know?"

Collis shook his head. "The voice that spilled the information on the phone was a man's, that's all."

"Bouche or Hansen?"

"Appears that way." Collis shrugged. "Or maybe this Roqué gal got someone to make the phone call for her, in case the word leaked out that one of them was playing it both ways. The other two might not like that."

"Are you sure Hansen is one of them? That's important, Cap."

Collis cocked his head to one side. "A funny thing happened after lunch today. On a hunch I had my girl Annie—you remember Annie." He winked. "I had her call a certain detective-inspector I know down at New Scotland Yard. It seems that about nine thirty this morning a very cool gentleman with a nice smile and a Mauser pistol

walked into the Holland and Holland shop over there on
Bruton Street. When he walked out again, you know what
he took with him?"

Locken's eyes remained steady on Cap Collis.

"A nice new .300 H and H Magnum with a Redfield
variable power scope. And that ain't all. Add a nine-thou-
sand-dollar Westley Richards double-barrel rifle, caliber
.458." Then Collis laughed.

"You think that's funny."

"Hell yes, I think it's funny. You don't see a lot of rhino
around London these days, now do you?"

4

COLLIS SLAPPED his thighs, stood up, and began pacing nervously.

"I don't know, Mike. Maybe I made a mistake coming here. Maybe I'm getting soft, just thinking what I'm thinking."

Locken swirled the whiskey around in his glass. "About me shepherding Nyoka out of the country?"

Collis stopped, stared at Locken hard, then nodded. "I guarantee you one thing. Anyone close to Nyoka will get within shooting distance of Hansen, I guarantee you that. Of course with those rifles, that might be about five hundred yards." Collis grinned broadly at Locken. "That is, unless this Bouche blows the lot of you up first. Or maybe Elise gets close enough to do some stunt."

"I thought one of them was supposed to make sure that doesn't happen."

Cap Collis paced again, staring down at his feet. "I hope so, Mike. I do indeed. What I want to know is, Can you handle it?" He stopped for a second time and examined Locken as though the answer would be found on his face, although he knew better.

Locken's face was impassive. "What do you think?"

"I think you were once the best man I had. I think a person gets rusty fast, even when the body's in good shape. You get careless, you don't see things. Just that much hesitation"—Collis pinched a finger and thumb together and sighted through them at Locken—"and you'll have had it." He stopped at the table and stared at the bottle of whiskey.

"I can handle it."

"Can you?" Collis's movement was quick for a man of his apparent softness. The bottle of whiskey arced toward Locken, hanging an instant at its apogee. Locken stood flat-footed, blinked, and instinctively reached for it with his right hand. The bottle bounced from his stiff outstretched fingers and crashed to the floor in splinters. Both men watched the stain that spread, looking altogether too much like something they both knew wasn't whiskey.

"Just proving a point," said Cap Collis.

"Next time bring your own example."

The door to the bedroom jerked open. "What in hell is going on?" Liz said angrily, looking from Collis to Locken. "What's the matter with you two?"

"You know what scares me, Mike?" Cap Collis frowned.

"Being alone in the dark."

"I'm serious now."

The door to the bedroom went shut with a window-jarring smack.

"This, Mike, more than the body." Cap Collis tapped the side of his head. "That's why you were so good. You didn't give a damn about anyone but yourself, and I know that included me."

"It showed, did it?"

"I mean that. You were a real pro and I admired that. I don't know what the hell came over you."

"What's that supposed to mean?"

"Seeing you all settled and contented here. I seen this all coming, Mike. Somewhere that last year, since about when

Rachman hung himself, something happened to you. You began to think too much, maybe. A pro starts caring about people, he's in trouble." He shook his head slowly. "Maybe Hansen did you a favor, Mike. You're still alive."

"I'll be sure to thank him. I want him, Cap." Locken looked directly at Cap Collis until the older man began to shift uncomfortably under his gaze.

"I believe you do," Collis said finally. "Bad enough maybe to make up for a lot of other things. But you're going to need help."

"Mack will do."

"Mack!" The word exploded from Collis's mouth. "You're out of your mind."

"I'll need a driver, Cap; he's the best I've ever seen. And he's worked with explosives."

"And he is also fifty-eight years old. That's older than me. Sooner or later things start to go."

"Not behind the wheel of a car. I know what he can do."

Collis scratched his head, then nodded reluctantly. "Okay, you can have Mack. But I'm sending someone else along."

"Two's enough."

"Two isn't enough. Mike, let me do you a favor." Collis's voice was a hoarse plea. "The way Hyphen Smith tells it, Nyoka isn't going to jump at our offer of help."

"What is he going to do?"

"Now just hold on," Cap Collis soothed. "It may mean you have to convince him. I doubt you can even wave a gun with that gimp arm of yours, let alone shoot."

"The left was nearly as good."

"Nine months ago. Maybe it still is, but I'm not taking the chance. I'm sending a gun." Collis paused. "I got me a new boy."

"What's his name?"

"Miller."

"Never heard of him." The irritation was plain in Locken's voice.

"Now don't get yourself in an uproar." Collis smiled a lopsided grin. "He's something else, that boy."

Locken turned away and paced slowly, grudgingly admitting that Collis was probably right. About his own skill, perhaps even about Mack.

"Okay, we take Miller. But make sure he can follow orders. How soon can he get here?"

"An hour," said Collis without hesitation. "One thing, Mike. This operation is off the record. SYOPS officially won't be in it."

"I guessed that."

"If it goes sour . . ." Cap Collis didn't finish.

Locken went on brusquely, "We'll need things."

"Name it."

"Money, a couple of thousand in cash." Collis sighed, but nodded. "Three small radios, UHF. Something that will fit a pocket."

Collis began to grin. "Electronic stuff these days you wouldn't believe."

"Weapons. The Smith and Wesson for me. Mack will want a Webley revolver. I take it Miller is equipped?"

Collis gave him an assuring wink. "I told you, Mike, that kid is something else."

"I'm taking your word. Have him bring a list of departure times of all airlines flying out of Heathrow, Schipol in Amsterdam, and Brussels for the next twenty-four hours. Any flight that would put Nyoka in a country bordering Buwanda. I want to know his options."

"Can do. I'll even toss in a rotten photo of Bouche. What's on your mind?"

Locken's eyes moved quickly in thought. "The fastest way for Nyoka to get out of England is the most obvious. Buy a ticket and climb on a plane."

"You going to let him?" Collis was watching him closely.

Locken's gaze steadied. "Meaning do I realize that if I lose Nyoka I also lose Hansen?" Cap replied with a careless shrug. "Our friends are going to come to the exact same conclusion I did, Cap. Nyoka may not get the chance."

"Mike, I want to say this for the record. Your job is to keep Nyoka alive, not hunt Rickard Hansen. Now you remember that." Collis hesitated, then grinned and winked.

"I'll remember it."

The noise sounded deep within the house itself. Then it came again. "What the hell?" said Cap Collis, frowning.

"Try the phone in the desk drawer."

Collis blinked. "Let me get it."

He listened at the phone, grunting every so often, then slammed the receiver down without saying good-bye.

"That was Hyphen Smith being terribly apologetic, besides having a couple of fits. Seems Nyoka has decided to move. Walked out and gave Hyphen Smith's people the slip. Sorry, old chap."

Locken was silent.

"No sweat," Cap Collis beamed. "I have a couple of my own boys watching Nyoka on the sly."

"They better not blow it," Locken said quietly. "He's the only link we have with Hansen."

"They won't. Nyoka isn't exactly inconspicuous. And he's got to move. He has to get to Buwanda before Aman can squash things. I'll get back to you."

Locken nodded with his eyes. "Make sure Miller's here in an hour. I'll round up Mack."

At the door Collis turned and looked at Locken with an unfamiliar pinched expression. "You know Marlis went back to the States. Took the kids with her."

"I hadn't heard, Cap."

"Don't matter really. Nothing much happening between her and me for years." The older man smiled blankly. "Thought she might have written you."

"Me?"

Collis shrugged, an awkward jump of his shoulders. "Just thought she might of." On the landing he stopped. "You haven't lost your nerve, have you, Mike? I'm counting on that. I've heard when you get shot like that, face to face, it takes something out of you for good."

Locken's expression didn't change. "I don't know, Cap. We'll find out."

"Good luck, Mike," Collis said, the broad grin firmly back in place. "And don't worry about Miller. He's good."

"I hope so."

"He's something else, that boy."

5

LOCKEN FOUND Liz in the bedroom, her suitcase open on the bed amidst disordered clothing. She stood in front of it, her back toward him, wearing only a bra and panties with elastic showing through at the waist.

She pulled a dress quickly from a coat hanger and dropped it into the suitcase without folding it.

Locken walked past her to the window and looked out. A dull-gray wood pigeon fluttered onto the sill, ducked its head when it saw Locken, and dropped in a ball toward the street below. Cap Collis was just climbing into a taxi.

"I've taken a day's work, Liz. It's not going to change anything."

She spoke, still busying herself with packing. "I just glimpsed the dark side of your moon, Mike. I knew it was there, but seeing it shook me." She paused. "I'd like to go off somewhere for a while and think about you."

With someone else, the whole business might have been carefully staged melodramatics. Locken knew it wasn't Liz's way. She lived without apologies or pretexts of any kind. He learned it that first day they had met, a bright late-spring afternoon on the cross-Channel ferry from Calais to Dover.

Locken had taken the train via Paris from Geneva and the private hospital where he had spent the last three weeks of convalescence following the shooting. He had preferred the soothing monotony of the French country-side and the bracing Channel crossing to the abrupt, jar-ring tedium of air terminals and taxis. Liz was returning alone from a week in the south of France.

They had stood next to each other in the line of people waiting to have their passports and their businesses nosed into by an officer of Her Majesty's Immigration Depart-ment, both clutching the pink tickets they had been given without explanation or instructions. Locken had laughed at himself for standing there like a sheep, dutifully clutch-ing his ticket. She had laughed because he had laughed. Six hours later they were in bed together.

There had been one anxious moment. Even after a Swiss surgeon had patiently assured him that the three quarters of an inch difference in the path of an 85-grain cupra-nickel bullet had left at least one part of his life unchanged, there had been an instinctive fear mixed with his desire for the girl. The gentle insistence of her hands and mouth had swept it away.

The next day she moved in her things from wherever they had been. Locken hadn't asked. Nor had Liz about the fresh pink scars on his body when she ran her fingers across them. The months since had passed quickly.

"There's a reason for the dark side."

Liz turned toward him. Her face was strong, with high wide cheekbones and large pale eyes, a face not quite beautiful. "This Hansen. He's the one who shot you." It wasn't a question.

Locken forced a smile. "He's the one."

Liz turned her head away quickly, angrily. "I don't un-derstand men. I don't know why that should be such a surprise after all these years. But I do not understand the games you play or what makes you tick. I used to think the difference was a gland or two and a few hormones. But it's not." Her head shook again. "I don't know why men have to keep the score even, or what kicks that pig in there was getting out of the whole business. I don't understand one goddamned bit of it."

Locken laughed. When Liz's anger came it was all in a rush, the sudden fury of a wild animal.

At the sound of his laughter a tight moan began low in her throat and came out between her teeth at the exact moment she lunged toward him with a wild swing of her clenched fist. He stepped away from it and then she was in his arms.

He took her, quickly, roughly, on top of the bed covered with her clothing, heedless of the coat hangers, the pain, or anything. She fought him an instant then fought for him, her pleas loud in his ear, mixing with his own, then dying away together. "I hurt you?" he asked later.

"No, it was good."

Still later she said, "What was Elise Roqué to you, Mike?" When he started to protest she put a finger across his lips. "I heard. I know I'm not supposed to ask, our gentlemen's agreement and all. At the moment I don't feel like a gentleman."

"It doesn't matter. It happened about a century ago."

"Did you love her?"

"I loved lots of things then. Elise was part of it."

Liz smiled up at him. "I don't believe it. Mike Locken finally admitting that once he cared for something." Her chiding was careful. There was so much she was almost afraid to know about this man.

"That was nineteen fifty-seven, Liz."

"I was around, darling."

"I went to Cuba; because what was happening there seemed more important than lectures in English Lit. Not revolution, or a revolution. But *la revolución,* with all the accents in the right places. It was a magic idea in Cuba in those days, and for a while some of it rubbed off on me."

"What happened?"

Locken paused, searching for the briefest possible explanation for something he couldn't put properly into words, given a lifetime. "In the Sierra . . . there were no more than a couple hundred of us. Fidel, his brother Raúl, Che, and a few others nobody remembers now: Valdés, Almeida, and maybe the strongest of the bunch, Camilo Cienfuegos. And of course, we, the faithful." The sudden self-mockery in Locken's voice surprised Liz.

But she asked evenly, "Elise was there too?"

"Oh, yes," Locken nodded, his eyes fixing on a distant point. "But six months after the New Year's Eve Batista climbed on a plane and that beautiful newspaper headline *Huya Batista,* things changed. The punks who waited on the sidelines to see how things would fall suddenly wore fatigues and beards and had stories about being with Fidel in the Sierra."

"No different than tales about Richard and Liz, darling. The other one."

"But when they started taking over I began to get a feeling. Then Cienfuegos died in an unlikely plane crash, and other things happened after that. I tried to explain to Elise why it wasn't good for me anymore. But the Havana police had killed her brother, not quick enough. She still had *la revolución* in her eyes. She couldn't live with it."

"What do you mean?" she asked gently.

"Love for us both, me *and* the revolution." Locken made a wistful shake of his head. "Elise made her choice known, I'll say that. Raúl was head of Cuban G-2 by then, and she told him I'd turned against them. One night they came for me. It's lucky the two I shot didn't die. I ended up in prison instead of against the wall. The Isle of Pines was quite a club in those days. Lots of faces from the Sierra."

Liz made a small sad sound and pulled closer to him. "What happened to Elise?"

"I never saw her again." His smile was bitter. "But I heard. Latin women have an instinct for survival, Liz, and Elise had the body to go with it. Let's say she was useful to the revolution."

Liz was silent for a long while. Then she said quickly, "I don't really care about her, darling. I want to know what happened to you."

"For three years, nothing. Then when Kennedy arranged the medicine swap for the prisoners from the Bay of Pigs fiasco I was turned loose as a friendly gesture."

"Three years." Her voice was a whisper.

"I was twenty-five and felt about one hundred years old. I weighed 135 pounds spread pretty thin over six feet of altitude. I had one aim in life. Get fat drinking beer in the Florida sun and forget about *viva Cuba libre*. Except Miami in those days wasn't any place to forget about Cuba."

"When you really want to forget, Mike, there aren't any good places."

"Ah, the voice of hard experience," Locken chided.

"Yes."

"Well, Miss Smarty Pants, I did. For all of three weeks."

"Well, I'm not going to feel sorry for you." She stuck out her lower lip.

"Neither did a clean-faced Washington type calling himself Jones. He bought me a dinner then cornered me in a Miami hotel room with a lot of talk about courage and idealism, ending his pitch with the suggestion of an organization in which I could nobly serve." Locken shook his head. "The words had that familiar hollow sound. If he'd come straight out and said they wanted a guy who spoke gutter Spanish and had used a gun, I might have bought it. Instead I said 'thanks, but no thanks,' and kissed the CIA good-bye. That was one good thing about Collis."

"I can't imagine anything good, Mike. I really can't."

"No speeches. He showed up a few days after Jones and offered me a job. No flag waving, no moral judgments involved."

"And you think that was a step forward?"

He replied sharply. "At the time, I didn't think anything. I'd done enough thinking on the Isle of Pines for a dozen men. I'd looked at myself and decided that the things we'd done in the name of the revolution were no different than the things Batista did to stay in power. The killing, the torture, they were all the same no matter what people said they believed in. No good guys or bad guys, Liz. One cause just as rotten as the next."

Liz's forehead furrowed slightly. "Do you still believe that?"

"Liz, something went out of me in Cuba." He saw the pained expression on her face, and laughed softly. "Well, you asked for it."

"I want to know."

"I stopped caring, Liz. About ideals, about people, about everything. Or so I thought."

Liz managed a weak grin. "Even I know that doesn't work, darling. I've tried. You end up a machine that walks and talks but doesn't feel. You have to care about something, Mike, or there's nothing to win."

The lines etched deeper in Locken's face. "I did. Until Hansen, I had something—a false God, maybe, but it kept me going. I had myself. My skill, in a not very admirable stock in trade. But I was good at it."

Liz laughed harshly. "Don't tell me about skill, darling. I lay mine on the line six nights a week, two shows a night, aware of every quarter note and quiver. Believing in the body isn't enough, Mike. Every woman knows that. Those cells change every nine years, and sooner or later the new ones don't have what you counted on."

"Maybe. I wasn't ready for the scrap yard yet."

"What do you mean?"

"I mean I still had it. That's why I want Hansen."

Liz lay back and looked up at him. "Well at least revenge is a good old-fashioned motive."

"Except it's not quite that simple." Locken moved up on his left elbow and inspected the mushroom-shaped scar on his right arm. "In the hospital I went over the night I got shot a hundred times, Liz. Hansen shouldn't have been able to do it. No footprints, not an alarm tripped, nothing until he went, leaving two dead men and a cripple behind."

"He managed it somehow."

"Don't I know it. Look, Liz," he said, hesitating. "What I said about not caring. These last few months . . ."

"Careful now," Liz said, eyeing him sidewise.

"I just might have started coming out of the Dark Ages. But there's a loose end dangling out there that's going to be with me the rest of my life unless I do something about it. Hansen is the only person who can tie it up."

"You're not exactly fit for the mile, darling. What are you going to do?"

Even as she said it she realized her mistake. Over the months she had witnessed in Locken a miraculous transformation, something she might have spoiled if she'd tried

to tell him. Slowly she had watched the layers of caution
peel away, letting the man inside come to the surface. The
lines of tension across his forehead and along the sides of
his mouth had softened, and he had begun to talk. About
little things, inconsequential things that together had
formed for her a mosaic of his life before they met.

Now he had told her more about his past than she
thought she would ever hear. And she had wanted still
more; she had tried to push him into the present. With one
question the caution had closed in again. The coldness she
saw in his eyes frightened her; he was slipping away, and
she hadn't the power to prevent it.

"I'm sorry, Mike," she said, sadness unconcealed in her
voice. She took a deep breath and sat up, the spell broken.
"I'm glad I was just your lover. I don't think I could have
handled this married to you." She grinned at him. "That's
supposed to be a joke." Then her eyes were filling with
tears. "Oh, hell."

She wriggled away from the hand that reached out for
her and ran into the other room.

When she returned Locken was dressed, waiting, his
face oddly expressive. He took her by the shoulders, almost shyly.

"Stay, Liz."

She shook her head. "If you don't get yourself killed,
you know where I'll be. Around. But not here."

"You're sure?"

"Yes I am, lover. Yes I am."

6

LOCKEN PAID off the taxi at the mews entrance and went the rest of the way on foot.

The street was narrow and unevenly paved with maize-colored brick. The small two-story buildings on either side had once been stables for the very rich, and later houses and garages for the not-so-rich. It looked to Locken the cycle might complete itself. Since the last time he visited Mack several more garages had become fashionably re-decorated "mews houses." From the window of one of them a face, effete though presumably male, sullenly watched him pass by.

Locken found the garage he wanted and looked in. A young pasty-complexioned man in grease-stained white overalls looked up at him from beneath a taxi.

"Mack around?" said Locken.

The young man glanced at his watch. "Will be, in about ten minutes. Wait in the office if you like. Tea in the pot."

The "office" was a plywood and glass cubicle in one corner of the garage. It looked and smelled to Locken like its counterpart might have anywhere in the world. Cup rings on a cluttered desk. The smell of stale tobacco and motor oil. On one wall, a calendar from a bearing company displayed a girl with a come-hither grin, unlikely proportions, and air-brushed nipples.

Next to it was a grainy black-and-white photo of Patrick "Mack" MacKinney sitting in the Offy-powered Blue Burd Special, in which he placed behind Wilbur Shaw's Boyle Maserati two years running in the Indy 500 of thirty-nine and forty. Burd, Mack once explained, was the name of the piston ring manufacturer who owned the car.

Locken recognized the expression on Mack's face. The single sober look with which Mack expressed everything from rage to amusement. Locken had never known Mack to laugh aloud, let his considerable Scottish temper run loose, or raise his voice. Mack was unflappable. Heredity, four years of bomb disposal during World War II, professional racing topped by more than twenty years behind the wheel of a London taxi; all of it had seemed to steel Mack's nerves beyond reach.

Locken had used the dour Scot a dozen times since the day, five years before, when Mack walked into SYOPS's office, announced in his usual direct manner that he knew what their game was, and said he wanted to drive.

Cap Collis had blinked, then laughed aloud. He asked Mack why.

"Bored," said Mack phlegmatically. "Plain bored."

Locken remembered the last time he had used Mack very clearly. The drive to Surrey with Wrodny.

Locken poured himself a cup of tea and looked at his watch. It was three thirty, less than an hour since Cap Collis had turned his world upside down with the name of Rickard Hansen.

He tried to avoid thinking how he would put it right again if Cap Collis's people lost Nyoka. Or if Hansen and the others found him first. Locken tried not to think about that or about the last question Collis had tossed at him from the stairs.

Locken had known people with blind courage and seemingly limitless nerve; he had seen it undervalued and squandered, and human life often wasted because of it. Locken knew his own nerve was a carefully manufactured commodity. The cold, aloof precision others attributed to him had been constructed by a rigorous self-testing, a continual probing of his limits, until with agonizing gradualness he had learned precisely how good he was. His nerve was built on that knowledge. How much the clear remembrance of three bullets tearing into his flesh and destroyed the construction was the question. The first sound of gunfire at close range would be telling.

Locken looked up at the sound of a revved automobile engine and watched the taxi back its way into the garage.

"You don't look as bad as I'd heard." Mack pulled off the leather-palmed driving gloves. He made fresh tea.

He was fully as tall as Locken and as slender, with a weathered face, beaked nose and slight stoop, all of which conspired to make Mack look his age and then some.

"You don't know where to look," said Locken.

"That way, is it?"

"Not quite, thanks to a shaky hand."

Mack's eyes rested on Locken, almost affectionately. "You ought to have a rest, Michael lad. You're not seeming yourself."

"I've had a rest."

"Ah," Mack nodded. He spooned two heaps of sugar into his cup.

"I've got a bit of work. Interested?"

"I'm not working for SYOPS anymore, Mike." Mack brought the cup to his lips. "Too many new faces."

"It's not for SYOPS. It's for me."

"That might make a difference." Mack's eyes rested on the girl's nipples then slid to the Blue Burd. A shadowy look passed behind Mack's eyes. "What's involved?"

The question was direct enough. Locken wished he

knew. At its simplest, catch Hansen, make him talk, then
deal with him as the situation allowed. Locken knew he
would kill him without a second thought. Nyoka? If he
could also send Nyoka off to save his country or himself,
he would. But given the choice between Hansen and
Nyoka, that, too, was not in doubt. He owed Nyoka nothing; to get Hansen he would stake him out like a lamb.

But beyond that? An ambitious Deputy Director in
Administration and Finance once contracted a well-known
research and development outfit in Santa Monica, Cali-
fornia, for a threat-assessment study of exactly what was
involved in SYOPS' moving a man from West Berlin to an
established safe house in Virginia. Locken had admired
the typing of the 192-page document, even tried to read
it, and had foundered hopelessly on a vocabulary from
another planet. Task definition, perceived roles, normal
costs, crash costs, basic parameters, optimal duration.

A diagram of the operation looked like a plan of the
British Rail System in some future century. Exactly thirty-
eight steps had been designated as essential to the "critical
path," meaning, as Locken understood it, what it took to
get the client from point A to point Z. He had turned to
the conclusion of the study in frustration, only to be con-
fronted with the pat, absurd wisdom of men whom he
could almost visualize huddled in their air-conditioned
think tanks, reasoning out the logic of a world they knew
absolutely nothing about. In the field there were no experts, no model situations. You took each mission as
though it were your first one. The minute you thought you
knew it all, the next minute you or your client were dead.

Oddly enough there had been one point in the summary,
one word that had remained with Locken, and for that
reason alone he thanked those musty men and the tax-

payer's money. The point made was simply if the enemy anticipated any single step in the critical path, the odds against successful completion of the mission were increased. The anticipation of any additional step increased the odds against success logarithmically.

Anticipation was the key word. If Hansen and company were able to anticipate one single move on Nyoka's part, they would sew him up and be gone.

Locken looked up to find the hint of a good-natured smirk pulling at Mack's thin mouth, as though he had followed Locken's thoughts.

"In words of one syllable, I mean, so a grease monkey can follow."

"I've had a government education. But I'll try."

Locken explained about Nyoka, Aman, and the three Aman sent to Britain, keeping nothing back.

"Since when did you become the underdog's friend?"

"Since the gentleman who put holes in me turned out to be one of the three. The lady Roqué and I are also acquainted."

"Could be interesting at that. How do you want to play it?" Mack tossed out the question.

"Put Nyoka on a plane, maybe."

"Heathrow?"

Locken nodded.

Mack squinted at his watch. "Rush hour soon, which means plenty of muckin' about in the city, and another fourteen miles after that. Expect trouble, I suppose."

"Guarantee it. We'll have a Mr. Miller riding shotgun."

"Good?"

"Supposed to be."

"Explain the maybe?" asked Mack.

"It may not be so easy. Nyoka hasn't invited us yet, and I'm not sure what he'll do when we volunteer. That is if

Collis finds him. If he isn't on his way home by this time tomorrow, he may be too late. If those three haven't got close in half that time then they aren't the people I think they are."

Mack sipped at his tea. "Maybe the joker in the pack will see they don't."

"It's possible." Locken eyed Mack curiously. "You'll do all right on expenses, Mack."

"I'm not worried about money." Mack lowered his cup and stared at it.

"You're worried about something."

The shadow came back into Mack's eyes. "Just calculating what's involved."

"If you don't want it, say so," Locken said quickly. "Miller and I can handle it."

"The hell you say." Mack's mouth grew thin.

"All right, I'm a bad liar. I need you."

"Then let's stop the polite conversation." Mack put the cup down decisively. "What am I driving?"

"It's up to you. Something heavy enough to take it, if it comes to that." Locken held his gaze without blinking.

Mack thought for a long moment, then nodded. "What about Burt here?"

"Burt?"

"My taxi."

"I don't think it's the job for a hack."

Mack gave an impatient snort. "You're a little old to educate, but since you don't know a thing, Michael lad, come along." He led him out of the office to the taxi. "Burt is no ordinary four-wheeled vehicle."

Locken detected the enthusiasm that crept into Mack's voice only when he spoke of automobiles. "Looks like any other taxi to me."

"A London taxi is no ordinary vehicle." Mack's huge

fist thunked solidly on the fender. "Haven't made a production car that sound in fifty years. Burt weighs a ton and a half, but can make a 180-degree turn sweeter than Henry Cooper."

"What does that mean to us non-sporting types?"

"A nine-foot turning radius. Could have rolled Blue Burd easier than old Burt. Fuel tank tucked under the rear seat with lots of metal around it."

Locken was listening now. "Thoughtful of the designers."

"Wasn't it now? Take a look up front."

Above the reinforced bumpers was a rack of three spotlights. Another movable spot was fixed near the driver.

"Lucas, quartz-iodine," intoned Mack proudly.

"Afraid of the dark?"

"I like to see where I'm going," replied Mack. "The best thing about Burt in a run like this is fourteen thousand of Burt's cousins out there. We won't exactly stand out."

"Will it move?"

"Burt manages. That's no Austin diesel you're looking at. This, Michael lad, is a Winchester with a six-cylinder gasoline engine. I've worked on it a bit. It doesn't do too badly."

Locken recognized Mack's typical understatement. He nodded agreement. "Okay, Burt's on the squad."

The pasty-faced kid in the white overalls came out of the office. "Are you Locken?"

"That's right."

"Bloke on the phone for you."

Locken went into the office, shut the door behind him and picked up the phone. "It's a lie," he heard Cap Collis say. "Sherlock Holmes was a bloody American. I should have been a private detective."

"You know where Nyoka is, or don't you?"

"Hell yes. His daughter's place. Hyphen Smith should have had it covered. But Nyoka ain't alone."

"How do you know?"

"One of my boys wrung it out of some Pakistani grocer in the neighborhood. Said she'd just bought enough food to feed an army."

"He was sure it was Nyoka's daughter?"

Collis laughed. "He seemed sure enough. What do you want, an engraved invitation?"

"What's the address?"

Collis gave it to him. "Sort of run-down apartment house in West 10. The neighborhood's closer to Jamaica than Eaton Square. The gal's a do-gooder type. Been a social worker up there among the immigrants. I'll keep a man on the place until you get there. You won't see him."

"What's her name?"

"Femi Nyoka."

"Anything else?" said Locken.

"Phone me when you make contact."

"I'll drop whatever I'm doing."

"You know what I mean."

7

"MILLER?"

"That's right."

Locken took in at a glance the man who stood in the doorway of his flat. Collis's boy might have been something else, but Locken decided it didn't show.

He was twenty-two or twenty-three, a half head shorter than Locken, with delicate features, a short upturned, almost cute nose, and fine blond hair a little too carefully disarrayed. Tinted rimless glasses hid Miller's eyes. He wore a plain gray suit and a rumpled blue raincoat over it. The *Adidas* raquet case in his left hand hung heavily by its straps.

"My tools," Miller said, giving Locken an empty grin.

Locken had arrived at his flat only minutes earlier. While Mack waited in Burt, he had climbed the stairs again and made his own private preparations.

From the medicine cabinet he took three half-grain disposable ampoules of Novocain, their stubby needles sheathed in plastic. If pain in either his elbow or knee became distracting, they would at least take care of the symptoms.

Then he went into the bedroom, aware of the strange cold feeling throughout the flat. He realized it was emptiness, an absence of the filling quality the right person's presence can give a place. Liz was gone, as she said she would be. Locken had known it even before he put the key in the door. He put it out of his mind.

Not that it was easy. Liz had started to become part of him. But survival meant not the slightest lapse of his concentration. By sheer force of will he pushed the thought of her into the depths of his consciousness.

He switched on the radio, felt around for BBC 4, then went to the closet and found the small suitcase at the back. A four o'clock news bulletin mentioned the revolt in Buwanda after the daily report on Northern Ireland and an announcement of the Foreign Secretary's visit to Rhodesia. "In Buwanda today fierce fighting raged . . ." Locken listened long enough to confirm that no one had any more recent news than the first flashes an hour before. First quarter score, zero–zero.

From the suitcase Locken extracted the knife wrapped in oiled cloth. It had been made by a weapons laboratory in Maryland to Locken's specifications.

It was no more than a thin, four-inch, double-edged stainless steel blade, telescoped against a spring into a knurled brass handle. Pulling the knife from its abbreviated scabbard set and locked the blade in place.

Locken strapped the scabbard onto his left ankle, and slipped the knife into it.

He went back into the living room. Miller sat patiently, the raquet case across his lap.

"Come on," said Locken. "Time to go to work."

"Mack, this is Miller. Miller, Mack." No shaking of hands, just light nods of heads.

Locken climbed into the back of the taxi after Miller. Mack pushed the button on the meter and pulled out.

Locken gave him the address he had taken over the phone from Cap Collis. "Know it?"

Mack flicked him a bored glance and didn't bother to answer. Locken smiled to himself. "Okay, Miller, let's see what you've got."

Miller shot him a shy grin and zipped open the raquet case.

Mack made a left off Bayswater Road, then another tight left just past a yellowed pub improbably named *The Sun in Splendour*, and drove into the south end of Portobello Road.

"Take it easy, Mack," said Locken. "The police stop us and look in Miller's bag they'll think we knocked over an armory."

Locken took the ten one-hundred-dollar bills, slipped them in one pocket, and put the folded new ten-pound notes in another without counting them.

The three radios were Swedish-made Stornos. Maximum range two miles, and small enough for a hip pocket. Also, more fragile than Locken would have chosen. He had used them before.

"Cap says for you to sign this." Miller held out a slip of paper. It was a government cash voucher.

"Tell Cap to sign it himself, or do anything else with it he feels appropriate."

Miller grinned again, and Locken realized it was more a nervous tick than a sign of amusement. Miller had small stained teeth.

"Cap sent you this."

Locken took the small black booklet, opened it, and smiled at Cap Collis's foresightedness. It was a suitably tattered I.D. card, with a picture of Locken which he was sure he never resembled. The card identified him as a Detective Inspector of the Metropolitan Police Special

Branch. Locken knew that he would never fool even the greenest rookie for an instant, not the way he looked and talked. Still, someone else he might. Locken slipped it into his inside jacket pocket.

He picked the Smith and Wesson automatic from the collection of firearms in the case. For an instant it felt peculiar in his left hand, then too many years of familiarity erased any strangeness. He checked the clip, snapped back the receiver, eased forward the hammer and put the weapon in his left-hand jacket pocket, with the safety off.

Mack glanced at him in the rearview mirror. "Beginning to look like a baseball umpire."

"You worry about Burt."

"Just an observation, that's all."

Mack drove through the part of Portobello where the tourists came to look at antiques, expensive junk, and each other. Locken handed the Webley to Mack, who took it without comment.

"Never seen one of those before," said Miller. "In a museum, maybe."

"Do you have a first name, Miller?" Mack said, pleasantly.

"Jerome."

"Don't doubt the judgment of your elders, Jerome."

"I'd rather not be called Jerome."

"That's fine by me, Jerome."

Locken said: "You should have something else for me."

Miller handed him an envelope, still looking at Mack. On the back was a list of airline flight departure times, destinations, with points of embarkation for each.

"What about the photograph of Bouche?"

Miller shrugged. "That's all Cap gave me."

The omission angered Locken, but there was enough to
worry about. He glanced quickly down the list.

There were at least nine possibilities out of Heathrow
that night. An African Airways flight at six forty-five,
direct to Entebbe. An Alitalia flight for Beirut via Rome
an hour later. Then Pam Am for Teheran also via Rome
at ten forty. Add two BEA and one Air France flight for
Paris, an Iberia flight for Casablanca via Madrid, and a
midnight El Al flight for Tel Aviv. All except the first
could work, but would necessitate connecting flights.

Locken looked at his watch. Four fifteen. The African
Airways flight was the obvious choice. He stared out
through the window an instant, then looked around at
Miller.

"First chance, put that arsenal of yours in front with
Mack. When we pick up Nyoka that's where you'll be. I'll
stay in back with the guest of honor. Cap tell you who
we're up against?"

Miller's mouth twitched, looking a little less like a grin
than usual. He looked down into the raquet case almost
fondly.

In it were the three radios, a short lethal .44-caliber
Ruger Carbine, and a 12-gauge pump gun with both barrel
and stock sawn off to a minimum. Miller was some boy all
right, reflected Locken, if his tools meant anything.

"You carry a sidearm?"

"They're worthless," said Miller, at the back of Mack's
head. "Got one, though." He pulled back his coat to show
the snub-nosed Colt Cobra in his belt.

"Okay." Locken took a deep breath, settled back against
the seat, and tried to relax. Mack pointed Burt straight
north on the Portobello Road.

Past the underpass beneath the A40 motorway the seed-
iness became absolute poverty, and beyond the Little Sis-

ters of the Poor Convent the streets narrowed and crowded, the white faces among the crowd fewer and more desperate.

Miller sniffed, and wrinkled up his pug nose. "Horse shit. I smell horse shit."

"I was wondering what that was," said Mack, giving Miller a slim grin. He turned left on Goldborn Road and pointed. "That's it. The big building in the middle of the block."

"Drive past it," said Locken, sitting up quickly. "I want to take a look."

8

THE APARTMENT house faced
a solid row of council flats, square four-storied buildings
of consistent plainness. On either side of the apartment
lopsided three-floor dwellings extended to the end of the
block, with small shops on the ground floor. It was a
neighborhood of chipped paint and today's wash hanging
in the windows, of ten-year-old automobiles, ice boxes,
and meat on Sundays only.

On the front steps of the apartment house three black
men drank hard cider from bottles in paper bags, listening
to a small transistor radio. One of the men, with a hard,
muscular face, raised his eyes and followed the taxi as it
passed.

At the end of the street Mack slowed the taxi to let a
half-dozen boys playing soccer with a beer can separate,
annoyed. One, a smiling boy of ten or eleven, looked at
each of the men in turn, let the smile fall, and raised a
clenched fist.

"Goddamned kids," said Miller. He began poking in a
coat pocket.

"If you don't see kids in a neighborhood like this," said
Mack, "then you better worry." He brought Burt to the
side of the road and stopped next to a closed pub.

Locken looked back, studying the street. "Is that how
you figure it, Mack?"

Mack nodded without turning. "Except for one very interested bloke on those steps, it feels okay. People this poor can smell trouble if it's around. No one's smelled it yet. Our luck just might have lasted the limit."

"What's that supposed to mean?" said Miller.

He pulled a small soft cloth from his pocket and began cleaning his glasses carefully. The eyes of a night hunter, thought Locken: small, dark, quick.

"Collis's brains aren't all that special," said Mack. "Nyoka disappears. Sooner or later our friends wonder about Nyoka's daughter. You can bet Aman told them about her. When they do, they'll be here."

Locken's eyes moved from the street to the buildings then to the rooftops.

He said quietly, "I have a hunch one of them already is."

Mack's head swung around in question.

Locken gestured with a tilt of his head. "Take a look at this setup. Two dozen buildings within sight of that apartment house. Not a tree or obstruction. It's a shooting gallery."

Miller's face was scanning the buildings methodically. "Lots of windows, too." His head nodded agreement, a slender grin bending his almost feminine mouth into a crooked line. "It would be easy."

Locken said, "They've had nearly twenty-four hours to come up with a place for their first play. Say they guessed Nyoka was here. All Hansen would have to do is get into any one of thirty or forty flats, or on a roof, and wait. When Nyoka walked out the door he'd take him over open sights. End of story."

Miller stopped grinning. "What if Nyoka don't come out?" His eyes were hidden again.

Locken thought for a moment before he answered. "An

African Airways flight to Entebbe two hours from now is temptation enough. He'd be in Buwanda by morning." Locken frowned tightly. "The trouble is, anyone who looks at an airline schedule will come to the same conclusion."

Mack looked at Locken cautiously. "You think they'll try something at Heathrow?"

Locken returned the question with a contemplative stare. "They may not need to." His eyes moved back to the street. "We assume the action starts right here. Mack, how much time before dark?"

"Sundown in forty-five minutes," Mack said quickly. "No cloud cover tonight, so figure light for another forty-five minutes after that."

He frowned at the clear sky as though it were a personal enemy. Locken saw the shadow again behind his eyes.

"What else?"

"Fog, most likely. This is the weather for it."

Locken breathed a quiet oath, then determined to cope with the problem of fog when they came to it. When and if. He hadn't thought about the implications of fog.

"How much time to drive to Heathrow?"

"Under an hour."

"How much under?"

"Could do it in three quarters if I get playful."

Locken glanced at his watch again, calculating.

"Keep it a secret, Mr. Locken." Miller grinned at him.

The glasses seemed to hide more than Miller's eyes. Locken examined his almost adolescent face and wondered how much he could trust anything about Miller. He'd find out soon enough.

"Miller, if that apartment house has a back entrance I want you to find it. There's an alley we passed beyond the front entrance that looked like it turned behind the whole block."

"Then what?"

"Cover it. And remember Hansen is above you somewhere. Anyone who goes in the back door who looks wrong, use the radio."

Miller seemed disappointed.

"Mack, when we're gone, find a place where you can keep an eye on the street. Someplace where you can bring Burt up in front or along the alley, in a hurry if you have to."

"Now let me guess where you're going." The lines on Mack's face deepened.

"I'm going to talk with Nyoka. It would be easier if he cooperates. I'm going to try and make the conversation last until dark."

"On the assumption Hansen can't hit what he can't see?" said Mack dryly.

"Hopefully he'll get itchy and come for a visit."

"And just how do you propose to get in?"

"Why the front door, Mr. MacKinney. One person sneaking around an alley is the quota. I don't want this neighborhood to smell trouble yet."

Mack squinted warily. "It won't be dark when you go in."

"Hansen had a chance to kill me once, Mack. He's after Nyoka." Locken paused and grinned at Mack distantly. "Besides, I want Hansen to know."

"Might make him change his mind," Mack said, in a disgusted tone.

The grin stayed on Locken's face. "I hope not."

Miller shrugged jumpily. "What if Nyoka don't cooperate?"

"If nothing happens by dark we'll bring him anyway. I'd

like it peaceable. We're not exactly playing on home court."

Locken worked the pistol out of his pocket. He dropped it and the money into Miller's case. Then he picked out one of the radios, tested it, and put it into the pocket of his coat.

"Why you leaving the peashooter?" Miller's grin was nervous again.

"I might seem like a nicer guy without it. If I want someone to wave a gun I'll call you."

"I'd like that," said Miller.

Locken got out of the cab and walked back along the street studying house numbers every so often as though he were searching for a particular address.

He could feel eyes following his every move. How many pairs of eyes watching him from behind tattered curtains, wondering what the stranger, so obviously not one of them, wanted with someone.

Was there at that second a single eye viewing him past the reticle of a telescopic sight, one index finger the barest twitch from sending him into nothingness? A stupid display of bravado, Locken admitted to himself. Based on the knowledge that a shot at him meant a warning to Nyoka and a call for the police. And the single suspicion that Hansen, knowing he was in opposition, would find his appetite sharpened for the game. It was almost as though Hansen had invited Locken to play again, looking down at him that night eight months ago, offering his name before he had pulled the trigger a final time. Still it was stupid.

Locken sucked in a slow breath. He realized he hadn't taken a breath since he stepped from Burt.

At the entrance to the apartment house he stopped, the low conversation of the men on the steps stopping with him.

He moved up the steps unhurriedly and edged around the men; they made no move to make his passage easier.

Odors of urine and fried food hung in the small entrance hall. A window on the inner door had one pane boarded over, the door frame scarred and pitted by too many people wanting in without a key.

Locken looked down the list of names on the mailbox until he found the letters F. N. He noted the number. He hit the door frame near the lock with the heel of his hand. The door latch sprung. He pushed the door open and walked in without looking back.

The foyer was a dozen feet wide and half that deep, with corn-colored walls that had started out yellow, and red lino floor curling at the corners and gritty to walk on. Bulb snatched from light fixture. No elevator. To his right, a flight of stairs led to a landing half way to the next floor then turned and disappeared overhead.

From the foyer, beyond an arch, a narrow hall ran straight back the length of the building. Locken followed it, smelling paraffin. Come Winter, buildings like this gave the press all the "Family Death—Shock" headlines they could run, leaving the police to sort out who had been who among the charred remains, and who of them exactly had kicked over the paraffin heater.

He walked the length of the hall far enough to confirm a second set of stairs close to a back door that led to the alley. He turned and went back, aware of the undefinable background din that invariably went with too much life, living in too little space. The black man with the hard face was waiting for him in the foyer.

"You don't belong here, Mistah."

"Never said I did." Locken stepped around him and started up the stairs.

"A minute now." The lilt in the accent could have been to Jamaican, Bajian, or Buwandan. Locken's perceptions weren't that fine. He continued climbing, more slowly than he would have preferred.

"I said a minute." Locken stopped when he felt the gun press sharply against his spine. "Now you climb to the next landin'. But slow."

On the landing the hard-faced man moved around in front of him. His search was careful but unprofessional. Locken smelt fear, as distinguishable as cologne on a woman. Sweat beaded the man's forehead. Locken could have taken the gun, even with one good hand. "I want to talk with Nyoka."

The man found the small radio, and stared at it as though it were to blame for his fear. In one quick fitful move he smashed the radio on the banister. He looked up at Locken, his jaw working.

Locken smiled at the man. "It took me a lot of green stamps to get that."

The man pinched his way down Locken's legs, felt curiously around the knee brace, and stopped an inch short of the knife strapped to his ankle. He straightened and gestured with the pistol. "Up."

He pushed Locken into an apartment on the third floor front. The room was ten feet square, light by comparison with the drab gray hall; board and brick bookcases filled with paperbacks; four canvas deck chairs; a card table with four plates and the remnants of lunch; a feel throughout of precise orderliness. On the walls were posters of Che, Fanon, and Malcolm X. Two doorways led from the room. Near one was an old leather valise, and next to it a pair of gigantic black shoes, worn but well polished.

Moses Nyoka came through one of the doorways, filling the room with his bulk, and something more Locken sensed immediately.

He wore a starched white shirt and blue serge trousers

held up by braces. He was in stockinged feet, working at the task of buttoning a cuff, made more difficult because his eyes rested directly on Locken. Nyoka's left ear was nothing more than a small bud, shiny with old scar tissue.

His gaze remained steady, curious, and slightly amused.

"We have a guest, Joseph?" Nyoka's accent was precise and dignified, more English than most English.

"He was comin' here, M'zee. He had a radio."

Nyoka took it in and looked at Locken. "Who are you?"

"My name's Locken."

"And what do you want here?"

"To try to help you if I can."

"Was he armed, Joseph?" The hard face shook a No. "And what makes you think I need help?"

"You know as well as I do. We can put the time to better use."

The girl came into the room behind Nyoka silently. Femi Nyoka was nearly as tall as her father, perhaps twenty-one or twenty-two. A strong, slightly flattened nose, framed by wide cheekbones, the hair worn natural but cut close. Her eyes were black and very angry.

She looped the necktie around her father's collar from the back, and tucked it under.

Nyoka buttoned the cuff and looked at his watch. "We have time, Mr. Locken."

"Less than two hours before your flight."

Nyoka bobbed his head without surprise.

Locken said: "If I figured it out, you can bet someone else will."

Nyoka began working on the other cuff. "Whom did you have in mind, Mr. Locken?"

"The three people your brother-in-law sent to kill you."

Locken let the idea stand without explaining that one of

the three assassins was playing a double game. Locken thought Nyoka might know already. He realized quickly he was mistaken. His earlier assessment had been correct. Nyoka seemed totally unprepared for the whole business.

The gun was suddenly in Joseph's hand, his jaw working again. Femi Nyoka's face went taut with anger. Only Moses Nyoka seemed unmoved by the news, except to sigh in a way that signified to Locken that despite his size and the impression of immense power he was an old, weary man.

"Yes," Nyoka said finally. Then he summoned strength. "And may I ask how you know?"

"A man I used to work for found out from MI5."

"What possible interest could you have in the matter?" Only the curiosity remained in Nyoka's eyes; the amusement was gone.

"One of the three shot me eight months ago."

Locken felt the girl's eyes on him change.

Nyoka smiled narrowly again. "So you are not here to help me, or more accurately Buwanda. But to help yourself."

"It can work both ways."

"A practical man, eh, Mr. Locken?"

"I'm not interested in politics, if that's what you mean. Or politicians."

Nyoka watched him curiously for a moment. "The words come very quickly to your lips, but no matter. We shall decline your offer of aid."

Femi Nyoka looked directly at Locken, her dark eyes bright with hatred. "You see my father finds it difficult to trust a white man."

"There you have your explanation, Mr. Locken." Nyoka's tone was mildly condescending. "And a lesson in how to find people worthy of trust. If they are black, trust them by all means. White? Then not." He turned to his daughter and spoke harshly. "Don't talk rubbish, girl."

"You should distrust them," the girl fought back, "for what they did to you."

The merest twinkle crept into Nyoka's eyes. "Look what I eventually did to them."

"After prison and eight years of fighting."

"You make me sound like El Cid, Femi. I fought more with my own people than the British. I rather like the British, in fact. In Britain. I fought them in our country because they refused to let go."

"White colonialists!" Femi Nyoka said venomously.

"One has nothing to do with the other," Nyoka countered. "The Chinese are the greatest empire builders in man's history and they are reputed to be yellow." He nodded at Femi. "Your children, God willing, or your children's children, may find that out. I would have fought them as I fought the British."

"And do you trust the British now?" Her tone was mocking.

Nyoka replied evenly, "I trust men, not nationalities or colors. My brother-in-law is the color of tea, and I can think of no one I trust less." Nyoka's face became firm. "If we must talk of those unworthy of trust, we should start with our own people. They're lazy. They lack discipline. They're easily corrupted. My own people were responsible for this." He pointed to the bud of an ear. "Leaving me to die in the bush, sick with malaria. I was a child, a weakling." Nyoka's eyes focused on Locken with dark intensity. "I woke from a coma with the breath of *fisi*, the hyena, in my face. He had taken my ear and wanted my nose. *Fisi* has extremely bad breath."

Nyoka's laughter began deep inside, finally overflowing in a gigantic mirthful roar, his head tilted back until his laughter was aimed at the ceiling. Then his eyes snapped toward the girl and he bent forward.

"And you know who found me? A missionary. And schooled me? His wife. Both English and white."

Watching Nyoka's performance, it could have been called nothing less, Locken sensed the overwhelming charisma of the man. His changes of mood were infectious; his temper, his charm, completely under control: each used in measured amounts as the situation required, aware always of the catalytic effect he could have on people near him.

Locken watched, caught up, until Nyoka turned and spoke to him.

"But I'm sure none of this interests Mr. Locken. The ramblings of an aging politician, one who has no doubt been corrupted along the way."

Locken started to speak but changed his mind. He glanced at his watch then back at Nyoka. "I have a taxi waiting. And protection."

Nyoka raised his eyebrows in surprise. "I'm perfectly able to call my own taxi."

"You'd be lucky to climb into it," Locken replied. "If you did, you still have fourteen miles of city between you and the airport. Even then you won't be safe. Airports are easy places to work. The three we're up against are the best. Go alone, and you'll be lucky to get off the block."

There was a moment of heavy silence, while Locken's words were fully digested. Even Femi Nyoka's anger momentarily gave way to surprise. Nyoka said, with a question implied, "You have the sound of authority, Mr. Locken."

"I've had some experience."

"And suppose it were not *they*," he said, emphasizing the last word, "but *you* who were hired to kill me?"

"Then I wouldn't have tried talking you to death."

Nyoka laughed in delight. "Quite so. But I still intend to decline your offer. I have quite adequate protection, as you can see. A militant daughter, and two quite able young men."

Locken heard the sound of heavy footsteps and was already moving sidewise when the door crashed open, and another black man, who might have been Joseph's brother, wavered at the threshold then stumbled into the room. Blood drooled thickly from split lips, his nose bent at an unnatural angle. He took another faltering step then went forward onto his face.

"Matthew!" Femi leapt to the man, Joseph at her side. Together they lifted him into a chair. A moan came from deep within him.

Locken's eyes met Nyoka's. "One of them isn't able anymore."

9

MILLER CAME through the door way then, the stubby shotgun held low and tight against his hip. Locken had expected it.

In one quick step Miller was at Joseph's back, the barrel pushed brutally into the black man's kidney.

"Gun on the floor. Fast!"

Locken saw stubborn defiance flare on Joseph's face and knew what was bound to follow had not Nyoka seen it too. His voice cut sharply. "Oblige, Joseph!"

Miller looked around, speaking to no one in particular. "Nobody tries to give me a frisk." Then his attention fixed on Moses Nyoka. Slowly an arrogant grin spread across Miller's face, as though the sight of the huge African under his momentary control gave him pleasure.

"Friend of yours, Mr. Locken?" Nyoka's tone was accusing.

"Business associate. Okay Miller. Come in and shut the door."

Miller tossed the Smith and Wesson to Locken. "You may need this."

Locken sensed the change in Miller. His voice and moves were sure, the shyness gone absolutely. "Why, Miller?"

"A big Bedford trash loader just came in one end of the alley, moving this way. I tried to get you on the radio."

"I could have waited for the news."

He saw Femi Nyòka's eyes narrow in question. "They don't collect trash with trucks here. An old man and his son come by with a horse and cart."

"You see," said Miller. "Besides, I recognized one of the faces on the truck."

"Hansen?"

"Naw," whined Miller. "An East End gun. Hundred-quid-a-day man. Two others with him."

Locken realized then he had made a dangerous error by thinking there would only be the three to contend with. They would have had contacts.

He moved to the window, edged aside the curtain, and let his eyes move slowly across the rooftops, pausing at each air shaft, water tank, and chimney.

He was looking almost directly into the sun, low enough now to be bisected by the rooftops, etching their profile sharply and lighting the face of the apartment building brightly. Hansen would prefer shooting with the sun at his back. He had to be there; and then Locken admitted that Hansen didn't have to be there at all. But if not, then why the sudden arrival of three gunmen via the alley at their back? Something was coming. Before they moved, Locken had to know what.

"Give Joseph his gun, Miller," Locken said, and as he did he saw it. The outline of one chimney seemed to widen for the barest instant, then return to its former dimensions.

Locken stared at the chimney, willing to believe he imagined it. Then he turned away from the window, forcing himself again to trust his own judgment.

"Hansen's there all right." Locken debated the idea of going after him. Even if he reached the other rooftop, a chase would have been physically impossible. "The radio, Miller."

Miller was watching the girl without looking directly at her, his eyes, thought Locken, fixed on the swelling of her heavy breasts beneath the pale blouse as she worked over Matthew's face with a wet cloth. He looked up with a guilty grin and held out the radio.

Even as Locken raised it a transmission crackled through from Mack. "Visitors, Jerome, do you read me? Can't raise Locken."

"Locken, Mack. In Nyoka's apartment. Miller's here. Spell it out."

"A gray Rover sedan stopped down the block about twenty seconds ago. Three men wandering toward the apartment house. Suddenly not a kid in sight. Nothing."

Locken knew what it was, then. A contingency in Hansen's plan in case Nyoka failed to appear before darkness.

"It's a flush-out, Mack. Three others in the alley, and Hansen on a roof." Locken hesitated, thinking. "Stay put until you hear from me. When you do, you'll have exactly thirty seconds to land Burt on the doorstep. I want a warning when your three go in the front."

"Check. You've got about a minute."

Locken pocketed the radio and moved to the telephone in one step. He snatched it up, listened, and replaced the receiver, an arid smile tugging at his mouth.

He looked at Nyoka and spoke calmly and quickly. "Six gunmen on their way. Another on a roof with a rifle, waiting. I'll give you one guess for who."

Nyoka managed a shadowed grin. "The suitcase or the coffin, eh, Mr. Locken?"

"It looks that way."

But Nyoka was already moving, slipping into his great wide shoes, talking as he did so, his powerful voice demanding instant obedience.

"Joseph, help Femi carry Matthew into the bedroom."

"Yes, M'zee."

"Put him under the bed and tell him to be silent. Make him understand. His life may depend on it." His eyes turned to the girl. "And Femi . . ."

"Yes." She seemed rigidly expectant of what he would say next.

"You must come now. You won't be safe here."

"I know," she said.

Nyoka turned to Locken, valise in hand, and made a gracious bow. "We put ourselves in your hands. Reluctantly, make no mistake about it. Instructions please."

"We can make it to the roof," said Miller. "There's a fire escape from there down the side."

"The roof is out," said Locken. "That's exactly what Hansen is hoping for. Us on the roof, little birds all in a row."

"There are back stairs," Femi Nyoka said flatly. She belted a tan trench coat around her. She began filling a large green canvas handbag with things from a drawer.

"They'll have the back covered," Miller put in quickly.

"How many would it take?" asked Locken.

"Two."

He turned to Nyoka and Femi. "Now listen, and get it straight." The girl recoiled from the hardness in his voice. "We're going out this door, then right, along the hall. We'll go down the rear stairs one flight, then back along that hall exactly halfway. Then we wait. Some gentlemen are about to bust this place wide open. I don't know how many. Maybe they'll use the front stairs, maybe the back, maybe both. I'm hoping they won't stop one floor short and check the hall. Anybody in his right mind would be climbing in the opposite direction."

"If they do check?" said Femi.

"They'll be shooting. Get on the floor and stay there."

Nyoka's quick nod cut short a stubborn challenge from the girl. "And then?" he asked curtly.

"We go down the front stairs and out the door. We don't have many choices and anyone guessing might figure it's last on the list. By the time we do, the chauffeur will be waiting."

Miller was grinning in anticipation. He rubbed the shotgun absently. "Where do you want me?"

Locken spoke quickly. "I'll go first, with Joseph behind me. Then Nyoka, Femi, and you, Miller. When we start down those front stairs, whoever crashes this apartment is going to know it a second later. Watch the rear."

"I got it."

"Then let's go." At the door Locken found himself laughing quietly.

"Do we amuse you?" Nyoka asked.

"Not you. The poster of Che. I don't remember him looking quite that Christlike."

They waited along the second floor hallway in tight single file. An eerie silence had enveloped the building, an expectant void of sound, the mind-filling babble of radio and TV conspicuous by their absence. Locken could sense the shuffle of people behind locked doors, listening and waiting.

From the radio in Locken's hand came the single word "now." At the same instant he heard the front door open below them.

From the footfalls on the stairs, Locken judged there were two men climbing, not slowly, not quickly. Two of six. Three at their back. Five of the six, with one unaccounted for.

Behind him Joseph hugged the wall, the odor of his fear

reaching Locken's nostrils. Nyoka's face revealed nothing; he edged Femi behind his massive bulk with a push of his hand.

The two men climbed past the second floor landing without hesitating. Locken waited until the planks overhead began to creak under their weight. There was a moment of silence. Locken knew they were at the door to Femi's apartment, listening. Then it came. The splintering of wood as the two went in, guns in hand.

Locken said the word "go" into the radio, and led them quickly, heedless of noise, ignoring the pain in his left leg as he ran, focusing only on the stairs as he took them two at a time.

Locken was three stairs from the bottom when the man appeared. He came out of the ground floor hallway into the foyer crablike, a blurred impression of gray flannel and flushed rosy cheeks on a flat, empty face. Locken dropped to one knee, instinctively bringing up the pistol as the unaccustomed strain on his left leg urged an involuntary cry of pain from his mouth, mixed with the crack of a pistol as the man fired first.

He heard Joseph suck in a quick gasp behind him then felt the sudden weight of his body as it pitched forward, driving him against the banister. Locken tore at the limp arm hanging on his own left arm, dragging down the pistol he was so desperately trying to bring into play.

The man at the foot of the stairs danced lightly, shifting his aim. Locken was still fighting Joseph's bulk when the sound exploded inside his head.

The blast from Miller's shotgun caught the gunman full in the chest, the charge spreading almost a foot across. The man lifted and spun elliptically backwards like a rag doll with its arms flung out. He caromed off the wall, leaving a bright red smudge, and went down in a nerveless heap.

Locken shook loose of Joseph's already lifeless body even as Miller bolted past him, the Colt revolver in his hand.

"You're a big help, Mr. Locken." He bent over the gunman and shot him once in the back of the head.

"He was dead before he hit the wall," Locken said. He felt the words in his throat, his ears still numbed from the blast of the shotgun.

Miller looked up. "They're the ones that get up and kill you."

Moses Nyoka moved agilely to a position just inside the outer door and pushed himself close to the foyer wall, pulling Femi next to him.

His face showed no emotion at all, and Locken wondered how much death had surrounded the old man in his lifetime. Next to him, Femi leaned her face against the wall, her eyes on the body of Joseph, her color a sickly gray.

"Hush, girl," said Nyoka. "You'll see worse than this in your life."

Locken moved quickly to the other side of the door, looking back up the stairs, knowing they had scant seconds before the other two gunmen would be there. Where the hell was Mack?

The high-pitched whine of an engine answered his question. Locken looked out through the door at an angle to see Burt moving toward them at incredible speed. For an anguished second he was sure the taxi was going past them, when at the last possible instant it swerved, braked enough to climb a low spot in the curb, then streaked toward them along the sidewalk.

Even as Miller lurched through the doorway, Nyoka and Femi hunched behind him, Locken heard the heavy footsteps on the stairs. Legs appeared at the top of the stairwell. Locken shot once, carefully, the recoil of the automatic at once alien and familiar. He heard the yelp of pain and saw the first man pitch headlong down the stairs, both hands clawing toward his thigh. Locken waited a full second that seemed an eternity. No one else appeared.

"Don't dally, Michael." Mack's voice was miles distant. He took a quick breath, pushed his way through the doorway, and dived headlong into the taxi, landing heavily on Nyoka's shiny black shoes.

Before Locken scrambled upright, Mack jerked the wheel and with a bump put the heavy taxi back into the street, accelerating rapidly.

In the front seat Miller cranked down the side window, the shotgun gone. In its place, in his almost caressing hands, the short semi-automatic carbine.

"Three behind us, Mack. Three still in action."

As he said it Locken saw the trash van moving out of the side street not a hundred feet ahead. He watched transfixed as the huge truck stopped across the road, its massive outline filling the entire windshield.

At their speed Locken judged there was no way to avoid the crash. He instinctively braced himself against the impact, aware of an octave jump in the sound of Burt's engine as Mack pounded the clutch with a smooth double movement of his foot, down-shifting with effortless precision.

"On your toes, Jerome," Mack said evenly, and brought the taxi full around at a speed that seemed almost physically impossible.

As the taxi swept within inches of the van, Miller shot three times in rapid succession, the tiny dark holes appearing a foot apart across the door of the truck. The face Locken had glimpsed briefly through the windshield a moment before was no longer visible.

The taxi tore back along the route they had just traversed, Locken hearing only the straining whine of Burt's engine and the metallic click as Miller calmly fed three fresh cartridges into the carbine.

The second man was waiting at the mouth of the alley. Without needing instruction Mack had chosen the alley rather than risk the entire length of street, passing in front of the apartment house and surely under Hansen's gun. The alley entrance was a scant eight feet wide, framed by brick walls on either side. Mack slowed, carefully threaded the entrance, and was gathering speed again when the gunman stepped from behind a bright green gate on Locken's side of the taxi, not more than an arm's reach away.

As the man steadied himself, aiming at Mack, Femi Nyoka yelled a warning at the exact instant Locken snapped a shot through the window, the explosion deafening inside the closed taxi. There was a bump as the man was propelled forward, crashing with a sickening thunk into the side of the moving cab. An odd questioning glance flicked across Miller's eyes, then his head screwed around again, searching.

Mack took Burt into a sliding turn at the final ninety-degree bend in the alley, a sharp biting screech coming from the tires as he applied power even before the car was fully aligned again. Not twenty feet away, and above them on a fire escape, stood Hansen.

The rifle dangled loosely in his hand, his leg swinging over the iron railing as though he were caught unprepared. His forehead looked even higher in surprise than Locken's memory had allowed.

The taxi was past him before Miller could react with more than a muttered "Christ."

"Stop!" It came out as a crackly, dry grunt between Locken's teeth.

If anything, Burt seemed at that instant to leap forward,

Mack's attention focused on the alley exit rushing toward them at unbelievable speed and not more than a hundred feet away.

"Mack!" Locken suddenly thrust the automatic through the six-inch space in the glass partition, pressing the barrel against the back of Mack's head. "You'll stop or be dead as the rest of them."

10

HE LOOKED through the notch at the rear of the pistol's receiver, centering the bladed foresight on a point squarely behind Mack's left ear.

How much time passed like that Locken later was never sure, remembering only the deepening stubbornness in Mack's face and his seemingly heedless, rock-steady concentration upon the act of driving.

Finally Locken lowered the pistol. He took in a stunted breath, as though the draft of air might remove the thought that had anchored itself in his mind. He sat back and rubbed his eyes, aware for the first time in minutes of the people near him; the massive bulk of Moses Nyoka on one side, the tense sturdiness of the girl on the other. He was aware of pain. Pulsations of it emanated from his knee, moving along his left leg in curious rhythm with the sharper contractions in his right elbow.

Mack's voice, laconic and unruffled as ever, broke the ugly silence inside the taxi. "You can get better odds, Michael."

"I know. It was the wrong thing." He barely recognized the sound of his own voice.

"The right thing, maybe. Wrong place. We haven't seen the last of Hansen."

"No," said Locken. He raised his eyelids with some

effort to find Miller grinning at him over the top of the front seat. "Go for the airport, Mack."

Mack nodded without looking back. "Through Chiswick and onto the M4. Halfway there already."

Locken forced himself to order his thoughts once again. "What are you looking at, Miller?"

Miller stopped grinning. "I thought we handled that pretty smooth."

"We did. Just dandy. Three dead men, maybe four, and lots of bodies around to amuse people. Add a kidnapping of our guest here, because you can bet it will look that way to witnesses. When the police add it all up we'll be very special." Miller's mouth had pursed slightly. "We handled it real smooth."

"You just be glad I was there, Mr. Locken." He turned and looked out through the windshield.

"That's what you're paid for, Miller. Don't expect a 'thank you' on top of it." It was a remark made in self-defense, and Locken instantly regretted it.

Nyoka laid a hand on his arm. "The business was not of your making, Mr. Locken. I think we might explain things to the police very persuasively."

"You might," Locken snapped. "Of course it would take a day or so before they believed you." Locken looked at Nyoka steadily. "I'm game if you are."

Nyoka shook his head after a moment's thought. "Under the circumstances, impossible."

Locken reached forward and pulled down a jump seat. He sat facing Nyoka. "I want to know one thing. Why weren't you on your way days ago?" With some surprise he realized he was angry with Nyoka's unpreparedness.

Nyoka laughed quietly, rolling his thick shoulders in a shrug. "If I had known . . ."

"The revolt came as a surprise?"

"Not entirely. I've anticipated something for some time. A man of Aman's caliber could never rule Buwanda for long. This particular bit of defiance," he waved his hand as though he were trying to dismiss the revolt from his thoughts, "was unexpected. I knew nothing until Matthew and Joseph arrived this morning."

"Poor Joseph," said Femi Nyoka absently.

"It wasn't your idea, then?"

"Not at all. I'm an old man growing older, Mr. Locken. Buwanda needs more youthful leadership, hopefully with a greater reserve of vitality than I have." The thought brought an amused smile to his lips. "As you Americans might say, I was drafted."

"Nonsense," Femi Nyoka said, whirling toward him. "You're the only one who can really lead them."

Nyoka moved his large head around slowly. "Them?" He used the single word like a dagger. Locken sensed again the rift between father and daughter he had detected at Femi's apartment. "Not them, Femi. Our people. They think they need me to oust Aman. Nonsense. All they need is a little political organization and patience." Nyoka smiled at Femi wearily. "I'm afraid your generation lacks the talent for either."

"Why should they wait?" the girl said acidly.

"Because for Buwanda there is plenty of time."

"You were not patient."

Nyoka responded evenly to Femi's argument. "Because it was time then to take a step. Someday it will be time to take another. Aman will eventually fall whether I am there to help push him over or not. Time is on our side, girl, and probably history as well."

Locken said: "If you believe that, why are you risking yourself by going back?"

A look of detached amusement came into Nyoka's eyes.

"Words come from one's mouth, Mr. Locken. A long way from the heart, I'm afraid. I could ask why you risk yourself to help me do such a foolish thing."

"I explained it once. I have a score to settle."

"Of course."

The older man's steady gaze irritated Locken. "You never did answer my question."

"I'm avoiding the truth, I suppose." He smiled. "Let's say I'm vain enough to believe that the sooner I arrive in my own country the more lives I shall save. I'm afraid my youthful supporters have given me no alternative."

Locken caught the irony in Nyoka's remark. "And just supposing Aman ends things before you arrive?"

"Then I shall have a rather warm welcome. I have no wish to die a martyr, Mr. Locken, so I suggest we move with as much haste as possible."

Locken glanced away for an instant. "Do you have tickets on the flight to Entebbe?"

Nyoka looked squarely at him. "A single reservation."

Femi Nyoka murmured: "I have work here. Obligations. I can't leave.'

Locken understood then the point of tension between them. The girl had no interest in returning to Buwanda. Nyoka confirmed it, his voice heavy with sarcasm.

"My daughter considers herself a revolutionary, Mr. Locken, a rather fashionable occupation these days. She has the slogans, the attitudes, nearly everything except a feeling for her own land."

"That's not true. It's just that people here need me. . . ." The conflict between respect for her father, and what she knew him to be, and the stubborn willful defense of her own life tugged painfully within the girl.

Nyoka looked straight ahead, offering her no understanding. "More I'm sure than the people of a backward country which happens to be your own." He brushed an imaginary fly away from his face and turned to look out the window. "We have more urgent concerns, do we not, Mr. Locken?"

"We do."

"Then if you'll put me on that flight we can terminate our brief, not altogether pleasant relationship."

Locken nodded thoughtfully. "There are other ways to handle this. It doesn't have to be Heathrow now. It can be a train to Paris or a flight from Birmingham."

"At the expense of time," Nyoka observed firmly. "No, we'll proceed."

Locken moved around in the seat. "You heard the man, Mack."

Mack's eyes lifted to the rearview mirror and met Locken's with an unspoken question. A flickering look of understanding passed between them. Locken turned to look at Moses Nyoka stonily. "But we'll have to do it my way."

"First, the trouble isn't all behind us," said Locken, "and probably never has been."

Mack turned south off the motorway onto a four-lane highway designated the A408, which fed a steady stream of traffic the additional one mile to Heathrow Airport.

Ahead they could see the last exit before the tunnel that led directly to the airport's three major passenger terminals. Above the mouth of the tunnel a brightly lit sign in blue-and-white neon announced, "B.O.A.C. takes good care of you."

Beyond was the airport itself, the terminals already great panels of multicolored light in the brief dusk, and beyond them, clearly visible, the enormous tail structures of a handful of jumbo jets. Rising above the terminals in

the geometric center of the complex was the tower building, and atop it a beacon light blinked, now bright, now
blurry with the passage of intermittent patches of fog.

"What do you mean?" Femi Nyoka asked, her full
mouth turning downward. Locken studied her carefully,
recognizing the symptoms. The ordeal of the past hour
had finally caught up with her.

Even as Locken watched, the girl shook off the frail
look that went with the knowledge of vulnerability. Her
face hardened with resignation. Her father had been tem-
pered like that: under stress. At that moment Femi Nyoka
looked very much her father's daughter.

Locken said, "I mean the attempt at your flat was
Hansen's play. Bouche and Elise Roqué would only have
been in the way. My guess is they've been here from the
minute they had a look at an airline schedule. A one-two
combination, guaranteed to score."

"How could they be sure we'd come?" asked Femi.

Moses Nyoka stared toward the airport as though it
were some distant, unreachable continent.

"With us pressed for time, as your father pointed out,
Heathrow was the only logical choice. Unless Hansen was
able to . . ." Locken left the sentence unfinished, damning
his own awkwardness.

"Carry out my assassination," Nyoka said. "I've heard
the word before, Mr. Locken." Nyoka's voice was wry, the
twinkle of a smile again in his eyes. "How do you intend
to prolong my valuable life?"

"Put you on that African Airways flight, but via the
back door. Going through the terminal is too risky."

"Why don't we hijack it?" Miller said from the front
seat. His voice was in dead earnest.

Locken replied carefully, treating Miller with more patience than he relished. He was beginning to understand

just how short Miller's fuse was trimmed. "Because whatever we hijack has to land somewhere. Wherever it is there'll be a reception committee. Hijacks aren't exactly kept secret these days. Mack, what time is it?"

"Five forty-five."

Locken nodded. "Heathrow is a big, complicated airport, which can work for us or against us." He explained precisely enough for Nyoka to understand what he intended to do, but no more than that.

"I hope someone knows his way around," said Miller, uncertainly.

"I've moved people through it. What about you, Mack?"

Mack grunted. "As of yesterday I could keep myself out of lost-and-found. Of course the place could have changed since then."

Locken looked at both Nyokas. "I want your passports."

"Why, Mr. Locken?" Femi's voice was reluctant.

"Because I may need them for what I have to do."

"I'm not leaving, Mr. Locken. That is clear, I hope."

"Very clear, Miss Nyoka."

Moses Nyoka handed Locken a green booklet with a gold lion embossed on the cover and the words "Republic of Buwanda." Femi found hers in the canvas handbag and handed it to Locken quickly. It was the familiar royal blue passport of the United Kingdom. Nyoka glanced at it blankly then looked away. The two different passports told the story more clearly than anything either of them might have said.

The taxi dropped down into the tunnel. Miller gave a nervous laugh.

Mack frowned at him sidewise. "What's so funny?"

"That sign. About somebody taking care of us."

"Jerome, your sense of humor brightens my day."

Near the end of the tunnel a bank of fog lights suddenly lit the taxi in brilliant orange. A moment later, out of the tunnel, in a brief stretch of comparative darkness, Locken thought Mack had lost his way. For a moment he seemed disoriented, his eyes jerking quickly. But then he bore smoothly right, joining the river of Burt's cousins heading toward the departure building of Terminal 3.

"I'm going in alone," said Locken. "When I have everything arranged, Mack, you'll hear from me by radio."

"Until then?" asked Mack.

"Keep moving. That's the most important thing. Hansen isn't far behind. He's already missed once today and he's not going to fluff a second chance. There's a five-tier parking deck across from Terminal 3, and a dozen other places he could shoot from and disappear into the crowd without a ripple."

"What am I supposed to do?" Miller's mouth was sullen.

"Keep an eye open."

"For what?" He began the ritual cleaning of his glasses again, the soft cloth making small circles over the lenses.

Miller's impatient question niggled at Locken's own reluctance to admit he wasn't quite sure. He had no idea what Bouche looked like, or what form the play at Heathrow might take. He had to assume that Hansen had notified the others of his failure, and that Nyoka now had protection. Locken wondered what would pass through Elise Roqué's mind when she heard Locken was one of them.

In such a setting Elise might be the more dangerous threat. Anyone who could kill two men in broad daylight in a hotel lobby would find the confusion at Heathrow made to order. Yet the one paid to ensure Nyoka's safe departure would avoid contact if at all possible. Hansen's recent willingness to kill appeared to confirm Locken's suspicion. If there was a ring-in among them it wasn't Hansen.

That left Elise or Bouche. Elise.

"I don't know, Miller," Locken replied quietly. "But keep your weapons out of sight. If the police aren't already looking for us, they will be soon. All we need is an airport bobbie to get a squint at your arsenal and it's over for all of us. That is, unless you don't mind shooting an unarmed cop."

Miller shrugged and grinned, almost embarrassed.

Mack shook his head in wonder. "Jerome, you make me plain uneasy."

11

LOCKEN STEPPED inside the sliding glass door to the departure building and took in quickly the setting and faces around him.

Terminal 3 was in fact three separate buildings, arranged like the separate strokes in the letter "H." The first vertical stroke was the staff building: administrative offices, lounge, locker rooms and commissary, all strictly off limits to the fare-paying customer. The other vertical stroke of the "H" handled transcontinental arrivals. The departure building formed the bar between strokes.

It was a rectangular shaped building with a flat, innocuous concrete-slab exterior, which Locken guessed satisfied acoustical engineers concerned with Tannoy clarity and engine noise, and left the eye to grab whatever pleasure it could. The interior was arranged on two levels, one or the other undergoing "modernization" as long as he could remember.

The ground floor directly ahead of him was a high-ceilinged reception area: four long rows of narrow stalls, each more than faintly reminiscent of a racetrack starting gate. Three rows of stalls were given over to B.O.A.C., Pan Am, and T.W.A.; the fourth to smaller independent airlines.

Beyond the reception area stairs and an escalator led to

a mezzanine. Coffee shop and visitors' lounge looking down on the floor below and stretching back through a maze carefully human-engineered for processing jumbo loads of departing passengers: emigration, departure lounge with duty free shops, and beyond, the departure gates themselves and an observation deck. The building was crowded, the air stifling; Locken had never encountered it otherwise.

He found African Airways halfway along the row of independent airlines. He knew exactly what he wanted done, but withheld a decision on the approach until he saw the reception clerk. Three choices were at his disposal: coercion, bribery, and outright threat. He willingly would have used either, or all.

The clerk turned out to be a pert-nosed black girl who looked efficient and prideful enough in her work for African Airways to be an African herself, and therefore hopefully less able to detect the fact that Locken's gruff Yorkshire accent, used so well to advantage by a number of officers of the Special Branch, was as phony as the I.D. card in his pocket.

He leaned toward the girl and flashed the I.D. discreetly. When she blinked, Locken gave her a cold official smile and asked to see the African Airways station manager with some speed.

A moment later a moon-faced African in his late twenties with skin a café-au-lait shade of brown, dapperly dressed in navy blue, scurried toward Locken and introduced himself as Mr. Mweeba. He smiled pleasantly and asked Locken how he might be of service.

"We'll need cooperation, I'm afraid." Locken made no effort to make it sound a polite request.

He flashed the I.D. again quickly, saw a new look in Mr. Mweeba's eyes, and explained rapidly and in some

detail exactly what he wanted, omitting any explanation
of why. He'd never known a cop yet who explained too
much. He watched the frown deepen on Mweeba's face.

"It's rather an unusual request." Mr. Mweeba searched
Locken's face for added justification.

"Ay."

Mweeba shuffled nervously in the following silence. He
said finally: "Our standard procedure on these matters is
clearance with airport security."

Locken inspected Mweeba icily. "If this were standard
procedure, Mr. Mweeba, I would have gone to them, not
you. If necessary I'll take it to your superiors." The threat
in Locken's voice was scarcely veiled.

Mweeba's face became a little less pleasant. "The flight
boards in fifteen minutes. I'll have to hurry."

"Appreciate it, Mweeba. Letter of commendation in it
for you, I'm sure."

The idea didn't appear to give the station manager
much solace. He shuttled off, and returned several minutes later.

"All right," he sighed. "See the First Officer on board.
His name is Lowry. I'll have to notify the control post to
let the taxi through." He explained the procedure to
Locken.

When he finished, Locken nodded curtly and asked for
the location of the nearest intra-airport telephone.

"At the end of the counter," Mweeba pointed. "Anything else?" The question had a fragile quality, as though
one more extraordinary request would completely shatter
his carefully built world of standard procedures.

"Nothing else," said Locken. "And Mweeba?"

"Yes." He looked at Locken fearfully.

"Well done." Locken spun on his heel and walked away
stiffly, aware of an audible sigh of relief behind him.

Locken used the telephone to confirm one final bit of information.

He was putting the phone back onto the receiver when he heard the sound. A slight clicking of a tongue against the roof of a mouth. It came to him from another life, unthought of in more than a decade, but unforgotten.

His head went back. He found her immediately.

Elise Roqué stood at the mezzanine railing above him, not a dozen feet away. The raven hair was too familiar, the face dark, beautiful, but no longer soft. The full Cuban hips just a bit fuller under the tan skirt of a stewardess's uniform pulling tightly against the undercurve of her buttocks in a style born to Cuban women.

Her smile, part taunt, part promise, pulled him back across time, obscuring for a brief instant the knowledge of what they'd both become. He remembered the smooths and contours of her body, the extremes she was capable of in love and when she hated. Then it slipped away. Without changing his eyes, he was gauging how much time and exertion it would take to reach where she now stood. Thirty-five, forty feet to the stairs. An awkward, idiotic climb past indignant people, wondering what had gotten into the man, then back thirty feet along the front of the mezzanine. The smart money said draw quickly, shoot to kill, explain later.

Elise anticipated his thoughts, for even as he watched her the smile became wary, unsure. She turned hurriedly, stopped, turned back and blew him a kiss.

Then she strode past the uniformed attendant at the entrance to the departure lounge without a smile. A defiant tilt to her head seemed to say, "Question me and I'll think you are a foolish man." The attendant gave her an agreeable nod, his eyes following the swing of her hips as she passed.

Time. To follow her now would cost plenty of it. The reasons she risked declaring her presence raced through his mind, each canceling the preceding one in its greater likelihood. A touch of unreasoned Latin nostalgia. Warning. Or an attempt to decoy while the others made their play. Or in order to kill him.

There wasn't time to dwell on any of them. He reversed, and walked rapidly to the front of the terminal to avoid the absorbing effect of concrete and steel on his radio transmission. Mack responded instantly.

"They're here," said Locken. "Elise positively. Where are you?"

"Just passing the roundabout near the tunnel. Coming back into the terminal complex."

"Take the road to Terminal 3. Before you come to the staff building you'll see a statue of two gentlemen who flew the Atlantic."

"Alcock and Brown."

"Make a sharp left before. You'll see a small glass house with a sign saying Control Point Five. The guard will know you're coming. He'll give you directions."

"Miller wants to know what he should do. He's getting itchy."

"Tell Miller to buy a ticket for the observation deck, and to check the departure lounge on the way. Elise is wearing a tan stewardess's uniform. Let him take the radio. He'll feel naked, but his heavy artillery is to stay behind. And Mack?"

"Yes, Michael."

"Don't dally."

Mack was in the middle of an appropriate reply when Locken clicked off, slipped the radio into his pocket, and moved rapidly back through the terminal.

Ten minutes later he was waiting at the foot of the movable companionway stairs leading up to the open rear entrance of an African Airways DC-8.

"*The* DC-8," First Officer Lowry explained, grinning. He was in his late twenties, a Canadian with blond hair and eyes that wrinkled in the corners when he smiled, which was often. Everyone's model of an airline pilot, thought Locken. "Every other Friday they let us dock with the big kids. You picked the wrong Friday."

"How much time before boarding?"

"Should be any minute. The baggage is on board. That's the cleaning crew leaving now. They were late." Locken watched the orange-and-white van move away from the aircraft. A bespectacled, almost placid face looked at him emptily through the back window. "The caterers are still aboard with meals and such. We buy the service from Bo-ack. When they're finished we'll bring on the bodies and be off."

"You have an S.O.P. for explosives?"

"Bombs you mean? Hey, we're not T.W.A., you know. Sure we run all baggage through a fluoroscope check, and anything questionable gets opened. We've got security people tearing apart handbaggage, everyone does that now. But no dogs, sky marshals, that sort of stuff." He grinned lightly. "Flying's getting to be the easy part."

"What about stewardesses?" From the foot of the ladder Locken could see the observation deck. The range he guessed about 150 yards. Anyone boarding the aircraft would be clearly visible.

"What do you mean?"

"What kind of girls are they?"

"Nice girls," Lowry said, a little defensively.

"I mean black, white, what?"

"Kenyan. Black, coffee-colored, I guess. All from good

Nairobi families." He winked. "Only way they can get out from under daddy's eye."

"You know most of them?"

"Sure," smiled Lowry. "I'm married to one."

"One tries to board you don't know, whatever color, do yourself a favor." Lowry looked at him. "Call a cop."

An African Airways pickup truck arrived a moment later with Burt tailgating it closely.

Even at a distance Locken recognized Mack's sureness behind the wheel. It had already saved them once; his unflappable temper had averted another disaster entirely of Locken's own making. He was depending on Mack's talents and judgment too much, he realized. He remembered the last time he had taken another person's skill for granted. With the boy Eddie, and the price had been two lives.

Locken opened the back door of the taxi and leaned in. Nyoka and Femi waited expectantly. "When you go up the companionway ladder, do it quickly."

"You don't mean *me*?" the girl asked.

"I do. For now, do what I ask you."

Locken watched them safely aboard, then turned to Mack.

"You pass an orange-and-white van coming out here?" Mack nodded, frowning. "See if you can catch it. Take a look at the people who get out of it. A good look."

"For what?"

"I want you to remember the faces. See if you can find out if they're regulars. Snoop, Mack. Go against your Scotch grain." Locken glanced at his watch. "I'll see you at the staff building in ten minutes."

Mack was shaking his head as he drove off. Locken climbed toward the open hatch, swearing again at the man who invented stairs. Moses Nyoka and Femi waited inside.

Nyoka said brightly, "My congratulations, Mr. Locken. We heard a news bulletin in the taxi. My young enthusiasts are apparently doing rather well. Aman now holds only the government buildings in the capital and the military barracks. I should arrive at a propitious moment."

Locken listened without expression, then nodded along the aisle. "Go through to First Class."

"Whom do I thank for the accommodations?" smiled Nyoka pleasantly. "You know I've never in my life flown First Class."

Locken pushed aside the curtain to the First Class section. "Don't thank anyone yet." Lowry stood next to the open forward hatch on the starboard side, concentrating intently on a clipboard in his hands.

"I'm not sure I understand you." Nyoka's eyes were suddenly suspicious.

"Lowry?"

"Right here, Mr. Locken." He tossed him the pairs of white overalls.

"Put them on," said Locken.

"You're not serious?" Femi said, incredulous.

Locken's voice became impatient. "You weren't leaving anyway. I'm postponing your father's departure."

Moses Nyoka shook his great head. "I'm afraid not, Mr. Locken. For what you have done I thank you. I'm safely in this aircraft and I intend to stay."

"You're aboard," Locken snapped, "but don't think you're safe. Make it easy for me."

"You can't prevent me from returning to Buwanda," the old man said defiantly.

"I don't intend to. An Alitalia flight leaves for Rome in exactly one hour from Terminal 2. You'll be on it. There's

a connecting Ethiopian Airlines flight from Rome to
Entebbe via Addis Ababa. You'll arrive two hours later
than you would on this flight. I happen to think you'll
stand a better chance of walking out the terminal at the
other end." Locken hitched open his coat, exposing the
pistol. "Now don't make me wave this around."

"But why?" asked Femi Nyoka, unrelenting.

"Let's say I have a hunch about this flight. It's been too
logical right from the beginning."

Nyoka stood motionless a moment studying Locken
with unvarying intensity. Then without protest he began
slipping into the white overalls.

Femi Nyoka glared at her father, then at Locken. She
pulled off the trenchcoat, balled it angrily, and tossed it at
him. "Damn!" She stepped into the overalls, black eyes
staring straight through him.

The overalls changed the appearance of both of them
less than Locken had hoped. Moses Nyoka's latent power
remained undiminished even in workman's clothing.

Femi cinched the belt tight at the waist, and stood
hands on hips, saying "Now what?" with her body. The
narrowed waist emphasized the fullness above it in a bold
way the trenchcoat hadn't. Locken smiled. Femi had a
style. An angry militancy, maybe, but with it a flam-
boyance she couldn't keep down.

"What are you smiling at, *Mister* Locken?"

"That outfit. It's supposed to be overalls. Not Pucci."

A thawed grin tried to change her mouth but she held it
back.

"Ready anytime," said Lowry.

Locken watched Nyoka and his daughter climb down
the service stairs on the opposite side of the aircraft from
the terminal, taking seats in the caterer's van.

Locken paused for a moment before following them.
"You remember what I told you about stewardesses."

"Ask a man who owns one," grinned Lowry. "I'm the boy."

"What about the cleaners' truck?" Locken asked Mack. The entire operation had taken less than fifteen minutes. They were again in the taxi, parked among a dozen other vehicles in a V.I.P. parking area near the staff building.

Moses and Femi Nyoka sat silently in the back seat, overalls gone. In the distance they could just make out the green-and-tan tail markings of the African Airways DC-8 as it made a ponderous turn toward a taxiway.

"Didn't find out a thing," Mack replied. "An airport security man waved me down thirty seconds after I saw you, and wanted to know what a hack was doing inside. God help you in this world if you're an outer, caught barefaced among inners."

"So you're becoming a philosopher."

"Happens when you drive a cab. I finally talked the gentleman into allowing me to park here while I waited for somebody I hinted was most important. Hence my special permission to join the inners for a few slender moments to begin with. Went snooping finally on foot."

Locken thought of Miller's arsenal. "How long was Burt alone?"

"Michael, I can't do everything. Ten minutes at the most." Mack squinted at him absently.

"Did you find the truck?"

Mack shook his head once. "Nobody seemed to know what I was talking about. Since I didn't know myself, I came back and waited."

Locken nodded silently, his eyes following the lumbering aircraft until it was lost from view.

Moses Nyoka tapped on the glass partition between the driver's seat and passenger compartment. Locken slid back the panel.

"And now, Mr. Locken?" Nyoka's impatience was un-concealed.

"We wait. I told Miller to watch until the aircraft was buttoned up and off the ground. "We'll pick him up in front of the departure building, then waste some time before the Alitalia flight."

Nyoka's displeasure was apparent but he sat back. Locken slid the glass shut.

"I'd be more comfortable leaving Jerome right where he is," Mack said. He made no attempt to alter the level of his voice. With the panel shut their conversation could be no more than guessed at. "He's a weird one."

"He's here to do a job. You don't have to like him."

"I get the feeling Jerome would be happier working for the other side. He doesn't much like playing defense."

Locken remembered his look of satisfaction when Miller had held Nyoka and his men at gun point in Femi's flat. He had been ready to kill and it would have mattered little who. "Thank your stars he's Collis's boy."

"Where do you suppose Collis picked up a stray cat like that?"

"I don't know. Maybe they're related."

Mack glanced at him sidewise, nearly smiling. "Nothing would surprise me." He looked forward, then asked: "Is what you told Nyoka about putting him aboard another flight on the level?"

"About two thirds of it."

"Which third is off?"

"There isn't a connecting flight out of Rome until to-morrow midday. I had to think of something to get him off that plane."

Mack made a low whistle. "Nyoka was on the verge of trusting you, Michael. Past tense."

"That's his bad luck," Locken said quickly. "We saved

his life once today. Let's say we're taking payment with a little time."

"You don't have to impress how hard you are, Michael. I'm old Mack, remember? I knew you when."

"Then don't you start going soft on Nyoka. My conscience is prickly enough without your stony heart turning into ice cream."

"I have my moments," said Mack. "I just can't figure why you didn't let him leave on that airplane. You got him aboard clean as a whistle. If those three believe he made it off on that flight they're going to disappear anyway, Hansen with 'em."

"Maybe." Locken's eyes searched the darkness. "Right now Nyoka is still the only bait I have for the trap. Besides, I meant what I said about that flight. It was too obvious."

"Well it got off, didn't it?"

"It looks that way. There could just as easily be a couple more Hansens waiting at the other end, in Entebbe."

"Some bait we have," Mack said, smoothing his thinning hair with a rough pat. "Me, I was never any good at baiting traps."

Locken looked at him sidewise. "Why not, dare I ask?"

"Usually snap my own fingers."

Locken smiled thinly. "And thereby, Mr. MacKinney, have you hit your head upon the nail."

"Glad to be of service. Of course you might explain what you're talking about."

"So far, all we've been able to do is stick close to Nyoka and react to whatever play those three made. It's been strictly defense."

"I'll settle for that," Mack replied lightly, but Locken saw that he was already anticipating his line of reasoning.

"Femi Nyoka's apartment. Heathrow. They were obvious because there weren't any other choices. Nyoka had
to come to them. Now, Mack, old friend, presuming of
course they don't fall for my feint of putting Nyoka
aboard that flight, they have no idea what we'll try next."

"And you do?"

Locken focused distantly. "I want a situation that will
bring them to us. I want a trap with limited approaches to
the bait, Mack. Working an airport or a city leaves so
many openings for a kill we could never anticipate them
all. We've been lucky so far. It can't last."

"That isn't exactly news," Mack said dryly.

"I need the right place," Locken said. "And I'm thinking hard."

"So am I," Mack brooded. He pressed the starter button, bringing Burt's engine to life, with what seemed to
Locken less than his usual enthusiasm.

Mack gave the blue-uniformed officer in Control Point
Five a friendly salute. He turned left past the arm-in-arm
statue of Alcock and Brown, then right toward the front
of the departure building. Locken knew that Mack's attention was on the automobiles around and ahead of them,
anticipating the possibly dangerous situation of being
boxed by other vehicles or forced to a standstill.

Locken studied the parking deck directly across from
the departure building. Anyone sitting in a south-facing
stall on any of the five floors would have an unobstructed
view of the entrance and the brightly lit street that ran in
front of it.

Next to him, Mack suddenly bent forward. He peered
across the top of the steering wheel, his eyes narrowing.

"Something's wrong," he said evenly. "Take a look at
Miller."

Locken turned toward the front of the building. Ahead, Miller was clearly visible, hands crammed deeply in his overcoat pockets, his head hunched down as though he were trying to pull it inside his body.

Mack snorted. "Inconspicuous as a shoplifter with a watermelon."

At that instant Miller picked them out and moved quickly to meet the taxi, the nervous grin fixed on his face like plaster.

He pulled open the rear door while the taxi was still in motion, letting out a sharp "Holy Christ" when he saw Nyoka and Femi. He jumped in next to them. "I thought you'd be dead."

Mack eased smoothly into the stream of traffic again. Locken turned swiftly, sliding back the glass panel with a sharp jerk.

"Explain it, Miller!"

"All dead," Miller said, pushing the glasses back on his nose. "Heard it coming down from the observation deck. "Took off pretty as a bird. I couldn't believe it."

"Believe what, man?" Locken fought the impulse to take him by the shirt collar and shake the words out of him.

"Over Surrey. The whole goddamned plane blew up over Surrey."

12

"GET US OUT OF here, Mack!"
The flat authority in Locken's voice did little to hide
the blind rage that rose up within him.

Mack spun the wheel sharply, turning out behind a
double decked B.O.A.C. bus cutting in front of them.

"I should have guessed it," Locken said tightly. "Elise
was trying to warn me it would be Bouche's play."

Mack said: "You sure read a lot from one gal's smile."
He cursed under his breath at the knot of vehicles stran-
gling the flow of traffic past the terminal.

"I could have come straight out and told Lowry he had
a bomb on board."

Mack looked at him. "Did you know?"

Locken shook his head. "I thought it was too high a
price. I underestimated them, Mack."

"Then what was to tell?"

Locken saw Mack's expression change. A sudden shift
of attention from his eyes to his ears, then an odd questioning look. Locken was aware of nothing that might
cause the change except that now, deep within Burt, the
tinny rattle of metal against metal.

Mack's look became one of complete certainty.

Even as Locken understood, Mack braked Burt slowly
with precise evenness, coming to a complete stop in the

middle of the lane of traffic. Behind Mack a taxi flashed its lights, and when it produced no response tentatively beeped its horn. Mack's lips drew tightly over his teeth. "Bomb."

The single, whispered word was unnecessary. Already Locken had reached around and slid open the glass partition, meeting the questioning glances of those in the back seat with a sharp demand.

"No one move. Not an inch. Don't even shift your weight."

Mack opened the door slowly, ignoring the insistent beeping from the taxi behind them. Locken sat without moving, knowing at that moment he was absolutely powerless to offer Mack help of any kind. A growing tautness gripped the base of his spine. His eyes darted quickly from building to building around them.

Whatever threat was at that moment beneath Burt, it was compounded by the fact that they had become a sitting target, the focus of attention of everyone within viewing distance.

Behind them the jammed traffic underscored the fact, sending up a steady discordant chorus from dozens of auto horns.

Mack was underneath the taxi now, his feet protruding, toes up, working absolutely alone on the task that meant life or death for all of them. When Locken looked up he fought the impulse to yell at Mack the single word "hurry"; the complication he most feared was wandering toward them at a controlled, but rather swift pace, the familiar blue uniform and domed helmet of a London bobbie.

On the floor at Locken's feet Miller's weapons remained in plain view. With his right foot Locken tried to ease them beneath the seat, only to find them blocked. He

freed the obstruction with his left hand, his eyes narrowing on the approaching police constable as he did so. At
their limit of concealment a good foot of each weapon
still remained visible—to anyone who bothered to look.

Without turning, Locken spoke to Miller. "Trouble
dead ahead. No matter what happens, no shooting."

"What's going on?" Miller whined.

"You're sitting on a bomb. Keep your eyes on me."

Femi Nyoka started to speak but was silenced by a
cutting gesture from her father. A thin ridge of perspiration lined Moses Nyoka's upper lip.

Twenty feet from the taxi the bobbie hesitated. From
his clearly recognizable insignia Locken determined he
was a regular constable; average height, a little soft in the
middle, with a thin blond moustache to disguise the fact
he was in his early twenties. Locken made up his mind.

Even as he eased his door open, the bobbie spoke
quickly into the microphone of the P.R. looped over his
lapel. Locken smiled inwardly in grim admiration. The
young constable had smelled something very wrong and
put in a call for assistance. Then he came on, Locken
knowing from that second the constable's strategy would
be a calculated stall until help arrived. He only hoped
Mack's task beneath Burt would be finished before it was
too late.

"Evening, sir." The bobbie touched his hat. "Trouble?"

His eyes moved lightly past Locken to Miller, Nyoka
and Femi before swinging back to rest on him.

Locken shrugged. "No idea, officer. I just got here.
From Cincinnati. Hell of a flight without this happening."
His accent came out as broadly American as he could
manage. "If you ask me I think the old boy just busted his
drive shaft. That's what I'd say if you asked me, although
I'm no expert, of course."

"I see," said the constable. "Perhaps we should push the taxi to the side. It's obstructing traffic."

"That's the right idea of course. But seeing how the driver is crawling around under this bucket of bolts, we better ask him first, huh?" Locken laughed with a heartiness he didn't feel. The constable stared back at him with practiced control.

At that moment Mack straightened up on the opposite side of the taxi, tossed something into the front seat, and nodded at Locken with his eyes.

He started to climb behind the wheel.

The constable held up a hand. "Just a moment." He walked around the front of the taxi, a little too casually, his eyes holding on Mack. It was confirmation enough. The young constable was more than suspicious. Now would come the drawn-out questioning. License, log book, insurance, destination.

Locken swiftly searched the parking tier looming over them, then back along the file of automobiles, ignoring the angry faces which glared back as though their every problem in life was his fault. At the rear of the file, perhaps a hundred yards away, a blue-and-white panda car came to a halt and two uniformed police officers stepped out and began moving toward them.

Miller watched him through the taxi window, then grinned as Locken nodded imperceptibly, hoping beyond reason that Miller would not misread the meaning of the nod and attempt to use his gun.

Mack had shut the driver's door and was pulling his documents out to show the constable when Miller stepped out of the rear door of the taxi. He stood motionless behind the constable, watching until Locken had circled the taxi and come up next to Mack.

Then without hesitation Miller moved. But even as he

did, the young constable was turning toward him. The pistol was halfway out of Miller's belt, when the constable wrapped his arms around the smaller man in a bear hug and drove him powerfully into the side of the taxi. The wind went out of Miller in a sickening cough.

"Mack!" cried Locken. The Scot took an easy step forward and knocked the bobbie's helmet off sidewise, exposing fine blond hair plastered against his head with nervous sweat. Locken hit him once carefully above the ear and felt his body go limp.

Miller scrambled out from beneath the dead weight of the young constable, an uncontrollable anguished whimper escaping his throat. Locken caught the wrist of his gun hand before it could move farther, twisting him roughly away from the unconscious figure.

For an ugly second Miller stood holding the snub-nosed Colt revolver, his face thrust toward Locken in defiance.

"I wouldn't, Jerome," Mack said quietly.

Slowly Miller grinned, his tiny yellowed teeth parted slightly.

Around them, wide-eyed faces watched in paralyzed disbelief. Locken turned his back on Miller and leapt quickly into the front seat. Miller tossed one look behind them, and still grinning, climbed hastily into the back of the taxi.

Mack ground the taxi into gear and put his foot hard down on the accelerator. Burt leapt forward.

On the seat next to Locken was a small rectangular metal box, with a length of braided nylon cord attached to a plunger, a heavy lead fishing sinker at the end. Mack had wedged a matchstick into the plunger, making it immovable.

They reached the single road that led out of the terminal complex, the tunnel visible in the distance, before anyone spoke.

"Close," said Mack, letting out a breath.

"In about half a dozen ways," said Locken. "What about the bomb, Mack?"

"Taped onto the exhaust pipe. That sinker was supposed to fall off the muffler when Burt moved, giving the plunger a jerk. When it did, a couple of hundred steel pellets would have exploded out of that box, punching a lot of holes in anyone enjoying the ride." Mack shook his head in self-recrimination. "Bouche could have done it when Burt was parked."

"We've lived through our quota of mistakes, Mack."

Coming out of the tunnel both of them saw it at the same instant. Ahead, less than a quarter of a mile distant, a file of three flashing blue lights moved rapidly toward them. Even as they watched, two of the three separated, the patrol cars sliding across the road.

"Roadblock," breathed Miller.

With bland nonchalance Mack angled Burt left toward the exit ramp that bent around onto the A4 roadway. The exit had been the last. A single second's hesitation on Mack's part, Locken knew, would have given them no choice but to try and breach the roadblock ahead. He said another silent "Thank you" to Mack MacKinney.

Moving west, Burt joined the heavy traffic making its Friday night exodus from London. They had left the artificial brightness of the airport behind, Locken thankful for the comparative dimness of city streets. Puffs of low fog divided as Burt passed through them, giving the odd illusion of great speed. Mack's hands tightened on the wheel.

"Funny thing about that bomb, Mike." Mack's voice was pinched and gravelly.

"I could use a good laugh."

"That lead sinker had fallen off the muffler all right.
But the cord was caught on the frame. The sinker was
dangling against the muffler; that's why we heard it."

"That's not even worth a smile."

"Shouldn't have happened, not if Bouche is all that
good. We shouldn't have heard anything." He looked at
Locken blankly. "Except maybe the singing of a few an-
gels."

"And I'll tell you another thing," said Mack. "We're
not getting Nyoka any closer to Africa driving in this
direction. Or haven't you thought about that yet?"

Mack delivered it with a sting.

Locken looked at him quickly, studying the uncharac-
teristic jumpiness that had come into Mack's manner.
"What do you suggest?"

"Go right around and put His Highness on that Alitalia
flight."

"Drive right through the roadblock."

"It's possible."

"Then sneak Nyoka on the flight without anyone seeing
him. Not the police. Not our friends, if they're still
around."

"Mike, chances are they figure Nyoka went up with
that airplane."

"That's why they put the bomb in Burt."

Mack shrugged. "Insurance, maybe."

"Or because someone saw enough to know Nyoka
wasn't on that flight. Half a glance into this taxi while we
were stalled in traffic would have confirmed it." Locken
looked out the window, an idea beginning to form. "Besides, Heathrow is swarming with police by now. Our
exploits of this afternoon have been pieced together, you
can count on that."

"How do you know?" said Miller, his voice defensive. "That young constable was suspicious the first second he looked at us."

"With Jerome leaving enough bodies to mark the trail it ain't surprising," Mack said irritably. He squinted across the top of the wheel. "Fog. Getting worse."

"Well, Mr. Locken," said Nyoka, heavy presumption in his voice. "What exactly do you intend to do?"

"Find a telephone, Mack. Let's see if Collis will send in the Marines."

The telephone box was in the entrance hall of a branch post office, the black lettering on the window advising that they had come as far west as the village of Taplow, just outside of London proper.

Mack had driven Burt off without question when Locken told him to get the taxi out of sight and post Miller as guard. Only Nyoka had frowned in wonder at Locken's continued caution.

"You'll find out soon enough," Locken muttered to himself.

He dialed the familiar number, and fed in a ten-pence piece when the party answered.

He recognized the clipped, competent voice of Annie, the leggy, rawboned Foreign Service staff officer who served as Cap Collis's administrative right hand. With the Vice President's arrival imminent, Locken knew he'd find her still in the office. Her tone relaxed when she recognized Locken's voice.

Once, early in his years with SYOPS, contact and a purely physical awareness between Annie and himself had resulted in an inevitable, but brief affair. There had been numerous like it in those first years after the Isle of Pines. He had pursued hungrily but without affection. The affair had run its harmless course, and following a few months of rather exaggerated formality had rounded into an even friendship.

It was via Annie that Locken learned that Cap Collis's locker-room attitude toward women had little basis in fact. Despite a marriage and two teen-age children Collis apparently had little interest in participative sex of any kind. When the urge did overflow, it came in the shape of an occasional liaison with a young man. Locken had been present in the SYOPS office when Annie had dealt with a particularly vicious phone call from one of the scorned objects of Cap's whimsy, and Annie, shaken, had told Locken angrily of her unwanted role as buffer, before she turned silent. She was too conscientious a professional to take pleasure in discussing Cap's private life; it was a subject that interested Locken not at all.

The theory, thought Locken now, might at least provide a plausible explanation for Miller. Since the airport, Locken's uneasiness had grown; he could think of few reasons why Collis would have saddled him with so reckless a gun.

Locken bypassed the easy banter which had become standard between them, asked a single, direct question, received a crisp, negative answer when Annie sensed it was business. Then he dialed Cap Collis at home.

Behind him Locken heard the door open. His quick glance caught the familiar stooped outline of Mack.

He heard Collis pick up the phone on the other end, just as a huge hand reached across his shoulder and slammed down heavily across the phone box, breaking the connection. Locken put the receiver onto the cradle and turned slowly.

Mack took a step back, his face gray and shadowed, the face of a stranger.

He stared at Locken fixedly, almost sadly, before he

spoke. "This is as far as we go, Michael. Any of us. I'm sorry."

Locken dropped his eyes from the lined face to the heavy Webley revolver held firmly in Mack's gigantic hand, aimed without mistake at the pit of Locken's stomach.

13

"You don't need the pistol, Mack."

"Neither did you today in the taxi. Seems we don't understand each other all that well."

Locken said nothing.

"I've got something to tell you." Mack moved the revolver barrel in a small circle. "I want you to listen, and no arguments."

Locken searched the weathered face, saw Mack blink in the faint light. He knew then the meaning of the shadowy look he had been unwilling to recognize earlier, the nature of Mack's private terror, clear for the first time. The spotlights; knowing the exact minute of sundown; his concern with clear skies and fog; the momentary disorientation driving from the tunnel into the air terminal.

Locken wanted to reach out to the older man, but held himself, knowing that Mack's pride would fight any gesture.

"What's wrong with your eyes?" Locken had to force the hard tone.

Mack gave a gruff snort. "Sounds like something you get from drinking too much gin. Degeneration of the choroid and retina, so says an eminent member of the medical profession. Isn't that a cutter?"

"How bad is it?"

"Bad enough and getting worse. Side vision might be through cotton." Locken remembered Mack's inability to see the gunman that nearly killed him in the alley behind Femi's apartment. "In the dark I'm no good to anyone, Michael," he shook his head with finality. "Not behind the wheel of a car."

"If you hadn't been behind the wheel today none of us would have lived until dark."

"It doesn't matter."

"It did to me."

"I thought you knew, and that's God's truth. I thought you were giving the morale a boost. A daylight run." He shook his head.

"How could I have known?"

"I thought Collis would tell you."

"Did Collis know?"

"I guess. The Embassy's been paying the bills."

Locken was silent for more than a minute. "He didn't say anything."

Mack straightened, the pistol steady in his hand. "Don't matter if he did or didn't. I'm not driving anymore. Not in the dark. Not in fog. I could kill you quicker than one of Bouche's bombs."

Locken knew arguing head-on against Mack's stubbornness was hopeless. "Agreed." He made a tired sigh and let the defeat creep into his voice, not unintentionally. "Point the horse pistol at something else, Mack. I have to think and my stomach in a knot doesn't help."

"As long as we understand each other." Mack looked down at the pistol and put it into his belt. He looked up, his voice a little softer when he spoke. "What are you going to do?"

"Get Hansen."

Mack shook his head slowly. "Forget it, Michael. The chance of them digging us out of this fog is exactly naught."

"We've underestimated them how many times, Mack? And how many times have we nearly got burned."

Mack squinted at Locken, then took a step closer, looking straight into his eyes. "What's going on inside there?"

Locken turned without another word and picked up the telephone.

Collis answered midway through the first ring. "That you, Mike? I've been scared shitless half the afternoon, I really have. If Nyoka was on that flight I'm damned sorry."

"He wasn't, but you can still be sorry. A lot of people were."

There was a long silence, before Collis said, "Now I know that makes you feel bad, Mike, and I can understand that. But I got problems of my own. What about Hansen?"

"He came a lot closer to bagging us than the other way around. Bouche nearly had us with a bomb at Heathrow."

"Where are you now?" Locken told him. "You keep a very low profile, Mike. You're in a fair amount of trouble."

"I was beginning to guess."

"You been the star of the VHF since that shoot-out at the girl's place. The police have an All Points out for Mack's taxi and good descriptions on the lot of you as armed and dangerous."

"Well we are."

"Now don't get humorous on me. This isn't a game of Monkey in the Middle, you know. It ain't kid's stuff. They're authorizing firearms for your apprehension. That's

polite British for 'They'll shoot you if they get a chance.'
You better keep moving."

Locken looked around at Mack. "That's exactly why I
called, Cap. I have an idea. But you'll have to buy a piece
of it."

Locken could almost see Collis frown. He fully expected
a short, crisp lecture detailing the reasons why SYOPS
couldn't get involved. He was mildly surprised when Collis said quietly, "I'm listening."

Locken said, "I want to lead our friends out of the city.
A place I know, and isolated enough to work without
interference."

"You know what you're asking?"

"Exactly. I want a killing ground."

After a moment Collis said in a new tone, "I suppose
you have someplace in mind?"

"The place in Wales we kept Rachman, with the old
longhouse."

Cap Collis chuckled to himself. "You remember that,
do you?"

"Like a bad dream."

"It's out of the way, sure enough. That country is
rough as a cob. It's also four hours drive from where you
are now."

"They'll follow us."

"You sound cocksure."

"I am. I have a hunch they know Nyoka wasn't on that
plane. They still want him, and they don't know what
we'll try next to send him home. Besides, they're tracking
us." Locken saw Mack's eyebrows rise slightly. "They laid
a beeper on us, Cap. I found it underneath the front seat
of Mack's taxi when I was trying to hide Miller's play-
things. Obsolescent stuff but good enough."

Locken nodded at Mack and took out what looked like

a cigarette packet from his coat pocket. Mack hefted the
weight of it solemnly and handed it back to Locken.

Locken continued. "Bouche must have planted it the
same time he planted the bomb. Figured to have us one
way or the other."

"Say they follow you, what then?"

"I'm not quite sure yet. Whatever I come up with will
have better odds than we're getting now. Don't forget, one
of their team doesn't want to play."

"You have any guess who?"

"It has to be Elise." Locken paused, not comfortable
with the sound of it. "The tries made by Hansen and
Bouche were both dead serious."

"Well now," said Cap Collis slowly. "You might have
some fun at that."

"There's just one small thing."

Collis's voice became wary. "I'm not sure I want to
hear."

"I'm putting Nyoka on a plane first."

Mack watched him, a flicker of a smile on his drawn
mouth.

"What!" shouted Collis. Locken moved the receiver
away from his ear. "You've just been telling me you'll
need him to draw those three."

"If we handle it right they might not know whether he's
with us or not. We'll put him on a train for Birmingham
when we go through Gloucester. Let him catch a plane to
the Continent from there."

Locken could hear Collis breathing heavily into the
receiver. "You could put him on a train, and he might sit
in Birmingham a week. Both Birmingham and Manchester are closed tighter than a pair of Scotch whores.
Fog, since about five this afternoon."

Without hesitation Locken said, "Then we'll have to
risk Heathrow again."

"Well now, Mike," said Cap Collis, his cheerfulness exaggerated, "there's no risk to it. I can guarantee you exactly what will happen. The police are crawling over Heathrow like ants. They'll want one helluva fancy explanation from Mr. Nyoka about a kidnapping and a couple of bodies left in an apartment building. They might not wait for an explanation from you. End up in jail and you'll never see Hansen, I guarantee that."

"I've thought about it."

"And maybe you thought fog was going to give London a break. Well it doesn't work that way. Heathrow will be shut tight before you even have a chance to make a hero of yourself."

He had thought of the fog. He looked past Mack toward the street. An amber halo surrounded each street lamp. It had worsened in the minutes since he had entered the post office.

"It's one of those nights and you're stuck with it," he heard Cap Collis say. "You got zero options." Then his tone became questioning. "I don't know why you're so concerned about Nyoka all of a sudden."

"He's in the way. His daughter's with him."

"You sure that's why?"

"What other reason could there be?"

"You know what I think. You get soft on Nyoka, someone will pot you."

"I haven't got time to listen. And neither have you. I want Nyoka out as early in the morning as possible and I want you to arrange it."

"Mike, if I told you once . . ."

"Near that old longhouse is a pasture exactly 760 feet long with one good clear approach. I'll guarantee it to the foot, because I paced it for the Rachman business. A chopper or something with STOL capability can make it easy enough. From that part of Wales it's an hour to

Brussels or Amsterdam and less than that to Shannon."

"I know all that. But I can't order aircraft like a cup of coffee."

"Pull a string, or dig up enough dirt to lever somebody. I want a plane."

Cap Collis started to protest. Locken cut him off.

"Five minutes, Cap. I'll wait here five minutes for you to ring me back." He began reading the telephone number slowly, and heard Collis scramble for a pencil. "Five minutes and we try Heathrow. No Heathrow and I just might drive Nyoka to Buwanda in Mack's taxi. I want him out."

"Christ, Mike," Collis said angrily. "With this business and the Veep due tomorrow . . . you know what pricks the Secret Service . . ."

"Five minutes."

There was a moment of silence. "I'll get back to you."

"Six and we're gone."

"Now Mike . . ." Locken hung up before Cap Collis finished.

14

He stared at the wall for a moment, then turned to Mack. "If we can get through the night without you driving, will you stick with it?"

Mack was squinting at him, puzzled. "Will you answer me just one insignificant question?"

"Probably."

"Do you still want Hansen or don't you?"

"I still want him."

"Then why did you give Collis the ultimatum about Nyoka?"

"Because it's a sure way to get Collis off his ass. For some odd reason he wants Hansen as much as I do. If he thinks Nyoka's presence will hinder my getting him he'll move."

"And that's the only reason?"

"You're as bad as Collis." Locken's eyes shifted away. "As of this minute, Nyoka doesn't stand a chance of reaching Buwanda in the next twenty-four hours. I'm trying to buy him a slim one."

"A chance," echoed Mack.

Locken turned on him angrily. "That's all he's ever had. He knows that. The odds have been longer right from the beginning than he's letting on. Fine. So we do him a favor and put him on a plane for home. If General Aman smashes that uprising before he gets there, he'll arrive just in time for his own funeral. Count all the African coups, rebellions, and uprisings in the last twenty years that have lasted longer than forty-eight hours, and you'll still have a couple of fingers left over."

"Then why are you trying?"

"Mack, I want Hansen. And that steely old bastard in the taxi wants to go home to Buwanda. If I can get us both what we want, I will. Nobody said either of us have to make any sense."

"Isn't there some easier way? For Nyoka, I mean."

"He'll have to fly. Either from here or the Continent."

"What about the Continent? We could drive to one of the Channel ports. Cross by ferry."

"So we drive to Folkestone or Dover. In this soup, two hours fastest." Mack nodded agreement. "And what do we find?"

Mack bit at his mouth thoughtfully. "I know what we don't find. Those fancy hovercraft will be snug in their hole until it's smooth enough to waterski to France and see the whole distance."

"And the ferries?"

"Don't know. One or other of the British Rail ferries runs in most any kind of weather."

"All right, say we catch the midnight ferry, either British Rail or Thorensen line. By maybe two in the morning we're in Calais or Boulogne or Dunkirk, with Paris another four hours by train—longer by car. All things considered, Nyoka might be at Orly by eight in the morning. Orly might be clear. And there might be a flight out of Orly landing within five hundred miles of Buwanda that I don't have on my list."

Mack picked at his head with a crooked finger. "Not getting any simpler, is it?"

"We'd be lucky to get off the boat."

"What do you mean?"

"Our friends were smart enough to check the flights Nyoka was likely to take from Heathrow. With the airports closed they'll peg the alternatives. One call to British Rail and they'll know all there is to know about ships across the Channel. Destroy that beeper and I'll tell you where someone will be waiting. On that ferry boat. It's the apartment house and Heathrow all over again. Us coming to them."

"We could decoy them. Lead them off with the beeper. Only Nyoka goes the other way."

"We could try. It might work. But if it doesn't, they'll kill him."

"I heard you telling Collis you could lead them anywhere."

"Mack, they backed up the play at the apartment house with another at the airport. They're not going to bet everything they have on a flickering needle and a hope Nyoka's at the other end. Someone will stick with us, and I'm betting on Hansen. But we don't know how many others are in on this kill. We've seen nine. Maybe there are more. If we fluff a decoy, and they catch wind of it, Nyoka's a dead man."

"He'd be safe with the police."

Locken hesitated. "I've thought of that."

"And?" Mack watched him closely.

"He probably won't go for it. It will mean forgetting about Buwanda." Locken stared away. "If that's what he wants, it's all right by me. We can probably draw Hansen without him."

Mack smiled.

"Now what's that for?" Locken snapped.

"You wouldn't admit it if I hit you on the head."

"Admit what?"

"A couple hours ago you were talking about Nyoka like he was some piece in the game. Plastic or wood you could do anything with you liked, as long as it got you your Hansen."

"What's any different?"

"The way you're talking. Nyoka has a value now and we both know it. Only I admit it."

"Mack, I'm just giving the old man a choice, that's all."

"Yes, Michael."

"And trying to get a straight answer out of you. Will you stick or won't you? Yes or no?"

"You're forgetting about these." A finger brushed his right cheek below the eye.

"No I'm not." He'd assessed it as coolly as he was capable of, trying to forget it was Mack involved. Night driving was out. In daylight he was as skilled behind the wheel as ever. But vulnerable on the periphery of his vision, and predictably uncertain in his reaction to quick changes in light. A suddenly darkened room, a change in the intensity of sunlight. Those were the question marks. Mack's eyes held him, making it clear without speaking. Mack would stick only if Locken kept him out of situations where he might be dangerous to others. There would have to be a silent contract between them.

"There's one other thing. About Miller. I want him with you or me, at all times."

Mack squinted at him. "If you're worried about him, leave him behind."

"I'm worried about all of us. I need his gun, Mack. He's fast but he's too hungry. That's why I want him close to one of us." Locken looked directly at him. "You see, you're a troublesome cuss but I can't do without you."

"In that case, I'll come. But it's your funeral."

"I'm sure you could have put it another way."

Locken was looking at his watch when the phone rang, five minutes and twenty-two seconds after he had hung up on Cap Collis. He heard Collis say without preamble: "Now listen, Mike."

"I hear you."

"If you start now you'll hit a village name of Cudwyp about midnight."

"I remember it."

"That farm is about another three miles along, except I don't know how you'll find it in the dark. You have to cross through property of a dairy farmer named Evans. Remember that if you get lost. At oh-seven-hundred hours an aircraft is going to put down on that pasture."

Locken smiled to himself. "Who's laying it on?"

"Now don't get too curious. I called that gentleman from Whitehall, Willie something-or-other. He thinks Nyoka is close to God Almighty, but if you ever give me another five-minute ultimatum I'll break your goddamned neck. Some people don't think that fast. Lucky I was talking about Nyoka and airplanes, seeing as those are the only two things I ever heard him make sense about. Pilot in the war, evidently. Said he'd have a plane there to scoop up Nyoka, by Gawd. That's the way he said it. Said he'd see to it personally."

"Can a pilot find it?"

"I pinpointed the exact position on an Ordnance Series sheet and gave landmarks. Any more and I'd be flying the goddamned plane myself."

"I meant if we still have fog."

"Mike, that's another country out there in more ways than one. Chances are there won't be fog. At least not by tomorrow morning."

Locken thumbed down the list of aircraft departures while Collis talked. There was a Japan Airlines flight due at Shannon at 0820 on its way to Beirut. And a K.L.M. flight out of Schipol at 1000 for Johannesburg via Nairobi. Either one would work. Locken favored the direct flight to Nairobi.

"But we'd be doing Nyoka a favor if we helped him miss his plane, I figure," said Collis.

"What do you know, Cap?"

"Only what anyone who listens to the BBC knows. Aman decided to get himself organized and fight back. Evidently Nyoka's people were already pouring out the celebration champagne. It may be a while now before they drink it. A lot of lead flying around Buwanda at the moment."

"That's Nyoka's problem," Locken said flatly. "There's an inn between Cudwyp and the farm. A big place set off in a grove of fir trees. Do you remember the name of it?"

"The Angel. Run by a guy named Belknap. Why?"

"I thought we might take a rest."

"Mention my name and lay a little money on him, and he'll walk on water for you."

"I'll remember to ask."

Collis was silent for a moment. "How's Miller?"

"He's the champ."

"Tell him to take it easy. Tell him I said just that."

"I'll tell him. If that plane doesn't show up I'll have a few things to tell you."

Collis laughed roughly. "It will, Mike. I have Willie something-or-other's word on it."

Locken hung up and spoke to Mack. "We'll keep quiet about your eyes. It won't make anyone more comfortable knowing."

"You have an excuse?"

"No excuse. Your face will be in a road atlas figuring out how to stay a jump ahead of our friends. There's a lot of road out there. When we reach Cudwyp we'll put up at the Angel and see who comes calling. I don't want to tip the site where that plane will land until the last second."

"Sounds like some party," the Scot said mildly.

"Don't it just."

15

A SULLEN Miller accepted Locken's order to drive, but without question. "Don't fret, Jerome," Mack said, slipping into the front seat next to him. He plopped the road atlas open in his lap and scanned it with a flashlight. "You're learning a trade."

"I already got a trade."

"Oh, Miller," said Locken. "Cap sent you a message."

"What'd he say?" Miller's tone was guarded, but in some small way pleased.

"He told you to be a good boy."

"No he didn't," Miller said quickly.

"I swear to God, Jerome," said Mack. "I heard it myself."

"He didn't say that. No crack about me being a boy."

"How do you know?" Mack needled lightly.

"I know." Miller smiled this time. Not the grin, observed Locken. A real, self-satisfied smile.

"If you say so, Jerome."

Miller didn't reply.

They were moving west on the A40, through thick fog, before Locken explained the alternatives to Moses Nyoka.

He spoke quickly and directly, first about the closing airports, the dangers of returning to Heathrow or trying the Channel ports, and that they were surely being tracked. Then he told him about the plane. "It's still a risk."

Nyoka listened without response, his thick arms folded across his chest. His eyes were half hidden by thick, drooping lids, and his features had gone slack.

Locken supposed he had heard the news about events in Buwanda on the taxi radio while he'd been on the phone with Collis. But there was something more.

"An airplane landing on a pasture?" Nyoka's tone clearly conveyed his doubt.

"We can put you at the door of the nearest police station, or on a train in Gloucester for Birmingham. If the fog lifts you might catch a plane for the Continent from there. But you'll be on your own."

Femi looked at him sharply. "How kind," she said, her tone brittle. Until then she had ridden silently, her strong face set with some private determination.

"In any circumstance I face delay," said Nyoka tiredly.

"It's your choice."

"As your columnist Mr. Lippman once said of two aspiring presidential candidates, 'Some choice.'" Nyoka looked at him, his next question measured carefully. "This man who has arranged the aircraft. Do you trust him?"

Locken was silent for a moment. "I don't completely trust anyone."

"Only yourself?"

"I even have a few doubts about myself."

Nyoka smiled with some effort. He shook his head slowly. "It's not enough, you know, Mr. Locken. You have to take a chance with people. Outside of God, they're really the only thing a man has."

"It's a nice idea if you live long enough."

"I've lived a modest number of years," Nyoka replied. He sat back and shut his eyes. "The blind must be led, Mr. Locken. We'll continue."

"You're sure?" To Locken the question was important.

Nyoka nodded heavily. "It matters little, one way or the other."

Locken couldn't understand it. For the first time Nyoka seemed ready to accept defeat, his sole defense an odd resignation to whatever might happen.

His eyes still shut, Nyoka mumbled softly in a language that wasn't English. Swahili, Locken supposed. He was somewhat surprised to hear Femi answer harshly in the same language.

Locken spoke to the girl. "What about you?"

"Don't be idiotic."

"Does that mean you're staying or not? An hour ago you didn't want to leave your apartment."

Her wide nose flared slightly. "I intend to see my father safely out of the country." She gave him a stabbing glance. "I trust you only a little less than those trying to kill him."

"Kill us, Miss Nyoka. You're not exempt. Not if you stay."

"I know."

She looked away again to leave Locken wondering what had happened. Both Nyoka and the girl had fallen into a mood Locken couldn't read, the difficulty compounded by their speaking in their own language. It had drawn father and daughter together, and made their separateness from him at that moment complete.

An uneasy silence enveloped the taxi, broken only by the steady purr of Burt's engine and Mack's frequent chiding commands to Miller, followed by the quick sway of the taxi as they turned to follow another route.

Locken pulled down the jump seat and sat facing Nyoka and Femi. He looked past them through the rear window. Along the road behind them he saw nothing, except the thickening fog.

The fog began to thin a few minutes after they passed over the Severn River west of Gloucester. By the time they crossed the imprecisely defined eastern boundary of Wales they had broken from the fog completely.

Mack slid back the glass panel. "That ain't good."

"They're staying well back. No headlights with us for more than ten minutes since Gloucester. If they catch us it will mean a free-for-all, and I don't think they want that."

"Maybe they're not there," said Miller. "Maybe we slipped them."

"Don't count on it."

"I wasn't meaning that," said Mack. He gave Miller instructions and watched him take a smooth turn onto another road. "Burt's a stranger out here. Suddenly he doesn't have any cousins at all."

Locken wondered numbly if there were other things he hadn't thought of. Collis was right. Without the habit of continual vigilance you lost the edge. Out of London Burt was a definite liability; few vehicles were as conspicuous as a London taxi 100 miles west of where it ought to be.

"I'll bet Jerome could steal us a car. Couldn't you, Jerome?" said Mack.

"I'm no car thief," replied Miller.

Locken had seriously considered the idea and decided against it. "Leave Burt and we lose the beeper. We'll be in the mountains in another few minutes. There won't be enough people to matter."

"I wasn't serious," Mack said, and winked.

Miller turned and watched him for a moment without expression.

The road signs now clearly marked that England was behind them. The names of every village and town seemed to proclaim the reluctance of the Welsh to be lumped with

the rest: Abergavenay, Merthyr Tydfil, Cynwel Elfrid. It
was old, tired country, the oldest part of the earth's crust,
Locken had read somewhere. In places twisted and bent
and eroded into an alien, discordant landscape, offensive
to Locken's eyes in its quiet hostility.

As they climbed into the mountains the air freshened.
Femi Nyoka dozed, her head on her father's shoulder.
Moses Nyoka's eyes rested on Locken, half shut.

At a distance behind them Locken watched the headlights that had flickered, sometimes disappeared behind
the configurations of the land, then reappeared at the
same distance. The headlights had followed them now
more than twenty minutes.

He worked his right arm, trying to will a greater range
of movement into his elbow. The strain on his knee from
the rapid descent of the stairs at Femi's flat had resolved
itself into a dull ache. He wasn't ready for the Novocain
yet, he decided. Not yet.

They had begun to drop through a broad pass between
two dark peaks, the Crug Bach and the Crug Gerwyllyn,
which Locken remembered from the previous drive to
Cudwyp with Rachman, when Mack turned, tapped on
the glass, and pointed ahead.

They were descending into a valley of a small river
named the Tyweli. Ahead was Cudwyp, the sight of the
village clear in Locken's mind. A small deadly quiet place
of a few hundred people who made their living shipping
milk to Cardiff and Swansea and providing the amenities
of life to the dairy farmers close by. Collis claimed they
rolled up the streets at noon. At that time of night Locken
had counted on Cudwyp being closed down and darkened.

Instead, ahead of them, the single main street was
bright with light, a large crowd of people moving as
though caught in a tidal surge, hanging in clusters around
the doors of a half-dozen open pubs.

Mack scratched his head. "It must be Brigadoon."

Femi sat up, trying to wipe tiredness from her eyes. "W' at is this?" Moses Nyoka said nothing.

"I don't know. Not what I expected."

"Can't we go around it?" asked Miller.

"There's not much to go around," replied Locken. "We're headed for a place named the Angel, a mile or so on the other side. Keep going, but take it easy."

Into the village proper, they heard the singing—powerful, but not boisterous, men's and women's voices mixed—the gusto in some way held in, restrained, like the Welsh themselves, it occurred to Locken. From a distance came the high tweet and whistle of an old-fashioned steam calliope. Femi gave Locken a questioning frown.

Locken shrugged in reply and looked at Mack. "I thought the Welsh were supposed to be quiet people."

"It's the quiet ones you have to watch out for. Isn't that right, Jerome?"

Miller didn't reply, but only gripped the wheel tighter.

Strings of clear white lights crisscrossed above the single main street, giving the faces and buildings around them a sharp, harsh clarity. At the end of the street, colored lights scribed the shape of a ferris wheel, and etched a rectangular carnival promenade. The calliope came from an ancient merry-go-round near the ferris wheel, its brightly painted horses galloping riderless.

"Slow down, Miller." Locken rolled down the window and addressed a knot of a dozen or so men drinking in the doorway of a pub. "What's the occasion?"

No one appeared to understand him. One man said something to the others and they laughed, then suddenly moved closer to the taxi, bobbing their heads to stare in curiously.

"Worse than the bloody Irish," said Mack below his breath. "They understand English as well as the Queen,

but don't think they'll let you know it. Their language is
the devil's own."

Locken repeated his question. An old woman in a black
dress and squat black hat, her cheeks heavily rouged,
broke through the pack and pushed her face in the taxi
window.

Femi shrunk back.

"Don't be frightened, darlin'."

"What's the celebration, mother?" asked Mack.

She smiled displaying perfect white teeth, grotesquely
incongruous as part of the coarse, painted face. "Cudwyp's anniversary. A thousand years. We've been here a
thousand years." She rolled her eyes at Femi, made an *oh*
of delight, and lost herself again in the crowd.

"Horrible creature." Femi breathed quietly.

"Now we know," said Locken. "Keep going, Miller."

The taxi edged slowly through the crowd, which neither
defiantly remained in their path, nor parted willingly.

"I'd feel more at home in Lapland," said Mack, casting
a glance behind them.

In the light from the carnival promenade Locken saw
that Femi's hands were clasped together in her lap, the
knuckles whitened. She muttered something to her father.
Locken saw Nyoka grin faintly; then the grin flattened
and he dropped again into silence.

A few moments later, in the distance Locken could
make out the Angel, ahead and to their right, perhaps a
quarter of a mile off through a thick forest of trees.

"Okay," he said slowly. "Stop here."

16

LOCKEN WATCHED Burt's tail-lights pull away from him, turn into the narrow drive leading to the Angel, and finally wink from view.

He glanced back toward Cudwyp; the road was empty. Then he struck an oblique course through the trees to-ward the inn.

He had been in the Angel once, drinking away the taste of Rachman's suicide without pleasure. He remembered the layout clearly, as he did everything that happened that day, as though etched into his mind with the detail of a fine engraving.

It was a square, two-storied building with parking be-hind, and a dozen or so rooms on the second floor. A properly antiquated sign over the entrance advertised that an inn named the Angel had stood on the site since 1541. He had been the only single male in the bar, the unusually amorous couples around him uncomfortable with his presence. The no-tell motel, Welsh style.

When he gave instructions in the taxi, Nyoka and Femi barely listened, as though the precautions concerned someone else. Miller grinned. Mack nodded, scratching at his head absently. "I don't need much beauty sleep any-way."

"After you talk to Belknap I want you inside the room

with these two, that horse pistol on your lap. Don't leave, understand?"

"Yes, Michael," he said dutifully.

"Miller, on the ground floor you'll find a bar and lounge. Stay in the bar until it closes, then move across to the lounge. If anyone asks, you tell them you can't sleep and give them that charming smile of yours. You'll be able to watch the front door and the stairway to the bedrooms. Shoot if you have to. But make sure it's the right somebody. Clear?"

"Sure."

Locken turned to Femi. "Do you have a scarf or large handkerchief I can borrow?"

She shrugged lightly and found a mauve-colored scarf in her canvas bag.

"What are you up to?" asked Mack, raising an eyebrow.

"I'll be out here with the owls. Two seconds in a bright light I won't see anything until it's too late. If someone wants to reach the Angel, they'll have to come along the driveway or cut through these trees. I'll be covering them."

"You really believe they'll try again?" Femi's voice held a continual challenge.

"If I were them I would."

There was a moment of awkward silence before Locken had stepped from the taxi into the darkness. Immediately Burt had jerked forward, leaving him standing alone in the road.

A dozen steps into the trees he stopped, listening. Traveling undistorted in the clear night air came a waltz from the steam calliope. The melody was familiar but Locken didn't know its name.

He tied Femi's scarf around his mouth and nose and breathed through it, taking no chance that his exhaled breath frosted in the low temperature might be visible. One lapse of any kind within sight or sound of Hansen and he wouldn't survive the night.

Among the trees the darkness was absolute. Without a clear sight on the Angel he would have been hopelessly lost.

Still it took him a quarter hour of shin bashing and toes mashed against stones, tree trunks, and God-knew-what-else before he reached the inn. Another five minutes to circle it completely, staying hidden in the trees except for a brief, cautious dart across the driveway.

It was nearly one before he found the place he wanted. Behind the inn, a stride from the carpark, between two trees growing less than a yard apart. Burt occupied one of a dozen or so parking slots. Locken checked again. Not a Rover among them. He looked beyond at the back of the inn, and to the left along the driveway that led to the road. His vantage point was as good as he could expect. He would have to trust the front door to Miller.

Even as he lowered himself onto the ground, he saw her and cursed.

Femi Nyoka moved along the driveway close to the side of the inn coming directly toward him. She stopped, looked around, her erect carriage giving the impression of some fine game animal trying to catch the scent of danger.

She slanted across the driveway into the trees not more than ten feet from where Locken waited. She stared directly at him, but failed to see him. She turned and started in the opposite direction, when Locken stepped forward.

He caught her around the waist and pulled her toward him, pinning her body against a tree. His left hand clamped over her mouth. "Only the village rapist."

She smelled musky, animal, and he felt her strong body tense against him, unchanging even as her eyes signaled recognition. He moved his hand from her mouth and tugged the scarf away from his face.

"I recognized the technique," she said tightly.

"You'll have worse damage than that in a minute." He pulled her down and drew her face close to his.

"I had to talk to you."

"It better be good. I'll wring Mack's neck for this."

"Some things a gentleman can't deny a lady. Besides, I pouted, and it worked."

"Femi, this business is for real."

"That's why it has to stop. You've got to quit using him, Locken. He can't take it."

"On that score your father and I understand each other. We all use if we can, Femi; and we all get used."

"There's very little left of him."

"More than you think, I'd bet."

"Physically, perhaps," she said. "I meant his will. It's strange. There's a whole part of him I don't know. Something that's still . . . primitive."

"It doesn't show, and wouldn't matter if it did."

"It does show. When we speak in our language it's as plain as anything. He's given up, you know. He's had some premonition of death. That's what he was telling me and why I had to come along. He swears he'll never see Buwanda again."

"You're not helping him any."

"You've got to stop this childish thing. Can't you take us to the place where the plane will come, instead of this?" Her voice became a soft plea. "It's so selfish, Mr. Locken."

"I can't chance it in the dark. When you see where we're going tomorrow you'll know why. Besides, you're no one to accuse anyone else of being selfish."

"I know," she said quietly. "He's right about me, and I know it better than anyone. Sure I play my games among the poor and have all the phrases straight. But I buy my clothes on the Kings Road, you can believe that. A fashionable revolutionary he calls me. He's right, and maybe that's why I fight him so hard."

"Then why not stop?"

"Because that means going home to Buwanda. That's all he wants me to do. The duty-to-my-people thing again. That's why he came to my place today instead of leaving straight away. He was trying to convince me to come with him. If he hadn't come for me he might have left before those killers arrived."

"Or he might already be dead. Why don't you go?"

"Because I'm afraid. In Buwanda there's no place to run when you get sick of poverty and disease." She laughed bitterly. "You see. He's right. I'm as phony as they come. He makes people see, Locken. That's why he's worth saving. People need him. I need him."

"What do you want me to do?"

"I want you to make him go to the police. He'll fight you, but force him. You can do it if you want to. You know you can."

"Put him in a sack, toss it over my shoulder, and carry him off."

In the darkness Locken could feel her eyes on him. "Please." She moved closer, her full, heavy breasts pressing against him. Her hand reached for his leg, then inside his thigh sliding up. Locken's emotional tautness had brought him close to the surface, primed. He felt himself harden immediately under the manipulation of her fingers. They moved to the zipper of his trousers.

His hand sought her wrist and turned it away.

"Girl turns on boy, boy promises what girl wants and gets reward."

"Would it be so bad?"

"It would probably be very good, but I've been known to promise things in certain horizontal moments I can't quite remember later. The beast with two backs is also the noisiest animal in the forest."

"I'll do anything you want."

"You wouldn't like it. And neither would I. Not ten minutes from now. If we were both alive." He took her by the arm, gently. "Femi, you don't need this. If we deal with the people following us, here, tonight, it will stop this crazy business. But you've got to help. And believe me, this ain't."

She pushed herself away from him and stood up. "I can do without the lecture." She turned, crossed the driveway, and walked quickly toward the front of the inn.

Locken stood motionless a full five minutes, waiting, trying to concentrate beyond the girl's words, her bargaining with her body to protect her father. He half expected a quick, silent try with knife or garrot. Nothing happened. No one came. He was still alone.

17

ALL OF HIS extremities con-
sidered, Locken discovered during the second hour that
lying flat on his stomach was the most comfortable
position, even though after ten minutes the dampness of
the ground had easily penetrated his body through to the
spine.

In that position he watched the Angel grow still, heard
the distant mournful calliope in Cudwyp abruptly cease,
leaving in its place a feeling of expectant emptiness. On
the second floor, bedroom lights winked on as the bar
closed, then off, one by one. Against the blinds of one
window not a shadow fell. Locken had forgotten to mention it to Mack, but Mack hadn't forgotten. Still another
window remained in total darkness. Which room contained Nyoka and Femi he had no way of guessing;
neither would anyone else.

He eased the automatic out of his pocket, thumbed off
the safety slowly enough to avoid the telltale click, and
waited.

Toward morning his head fell forward, striking the
hammer of the pistol, and bobbed up again immediately.

He fought the temptation to rise, to stretch the stiffness
out of his body. He was sleepy and bone cold. But he
knew Hansen could wait. Hansen's business was waiting.

He remained absolutely motionless, hoping he looked as much a part of the earth as he felt.

That Hansen would be one of those who would follow, he was almost certain. The business at the apartment house must have been a slap to his pride; and he knew now Locken was against him. But who else? If Bouche rigged the beeper, then in all likelihood he had the knowledge necessary to use the tracking equipment. If Elise's taunting smile at the airport had been a warning, if she was the double, then she too would find some way to tag along.

And still there might be others. Of the six gunmen from the attack at the apartment house, two were dead, the one in the cab of the trash loader a probable, the one Locken shot on the stairs definitely out of action. Two left of the original six.

Bouche, busy with equipment, would want a driver. Hansen wouldn't want his hands occupied, nor in all likelihood would Elise. That meant at least one other. If the full contingent had followed them in the gray Rover, that meant he, Mack, and Miller had five to contend with. Unless the original squad had been bolstered by replacements. A likely possibility, Locken decided.

Exactly when he no longer felt alone among the trees he never precisely determined. One moment his attention had wandered to Liz, to her fine, strong hips, fuller unclothed than they appeared. The next moment his hand was sweaty on the walnut grip of the pistol, the shock surge of adrenalin pounding through his system, his heart beating loud enough in his throat to be heard he was sure.

A second after awareness came confirmation, the sharp ammoniac aroma of someone relieving himself a few feet to his left.

Still he saw nothing until a thick shadow detached from

the trees and began moving toward the carpark with extraordinary nonchalance.

He was a big man, clearly visible in outline, wearing a lumpy top coat and soft cap. He strode without hesitation toward Burt, both hands stuffed deeply into the pockets of the coat.

Locken forced himself to lie still. Once raised from the ground he would be committed to act, and act quickly. The chance that the big man was alone seemed unlikely. Yet if someone else watched, they remained hidden, perhaps waiting to carry out whatever followed the big man's prelude.

When he came to Burt, the big man stopped. Harsh scraping of metal against metal as the gas cap loosened.

Locken glanced quickly to either side, knowing that without Burt they'd have to improvise transportation. They might not have the luxury of time. He pushed himself up, and went forward, his body in a half crouch, the pistol reluctantly ready. He wanted to avoid shooting.

The big man tossed the gas cap aside, and produced a bottle from the pocket of the bulky coat. Locken spoke, still ten feet away, in a voice barely above a whisper.

"Not another inch. Not one." The big man hesitated and started to turn. "Not that either. Bottle down, hands high, and lean against the taxi. Nice and easy."

Locken approached him from behind, the automatic pointing from tight against his hip.

"Now we're going to play a game." He shoved his left foot between the man's feet and kicked them apart easily. "I can see you've played this game before."

Locken searched him with his right hand, finding a revolver, a leathered cosh, and a cheap Spanish spring knife. The man had no I.D. Close up he smelt of beer and stale tobacco.

The man turned his head and looked at Locken over his

shoulder, the flattened nose red around the nostrils and visibly runny. The man sniffed.

"Give a stiff a break, guv."

Even as he pleaded, his right shoulder dipped with surprising quickness. He pivoted, bringing his left hand down across Locken's arm. The pistol spun from his hand.

Locken had tried to step back, but without natural movement in his left leg, his balance was appalling. He'd lost the pistol to a move that should have bought the big man a bullet in the kidney. Almost in the same motion the big man's right fist hammered up in a short, quick uppercut that caught Locken ducking his head away. The man's blow glanced off the side of Locken's head, above the ear, getting a fistful of hard skull. The big man gave an *Ow* of pain. Unable to step back, jab and kick, Locken stepped inside, driving the top of his head toward the smear of a face. The *Ow* changed to a loose gurgle as he felt teeth cut into his scalp, then break away.

One thick arm grappled Locken's neck, pulling him close. A fresh, coppery smell mixed with the pungent staleness of tobacco in his nostrils. Already Locken's hand was on the knife at his ankle. The big man's arm tightened on the back of his neck, as the knife came up in a half circle with his strength behind it. He felt the tip grate across bone, twist, then slip off into softness. The man started to scream.

Locken pulled loose from the arm, stifling the scream with the collar of the man's overcoat. He shoved him back against the taxi, and used the knife once, carefully. The big man crumpled and thankfully was silent.

Without waiting, Locken grabbed handfuls of coat and dragged him toward the trees. He continued pulling the lifeless form probably twice the distance necessary before he let the hulk drop.

Then he stepped a full pace, bent, and vomited noisily between his feet.

Miller looked up, startled. "Jeez, what happened to you?"

"I had an argument with a man. About adding sugar syrup to Burt's gas tank. Noisy enough to warn everyone I was around."

Miller sat alone in a darkened corner of the lounge, a copy of *Country Life* open in his lap.

"Did you kill him?"

Without answering him Locken went through the bar, found the washroom, and took a long time washing his hands and face. He used a wet paper towel to wipe the front of his jacket. He could still smell tobacco.

He went back to the lounge and faced Miller. "All right, let's have it."

"Have what?" said Miller defensively. One hand stayed beneath the magazine. His eyes, unhidden by glasses, moved continually.

"Everything that's happened since you've been here. I can't believe sugar in the gas tank is the best they can muster."

"Nothing's happened. I've been here all night. Just like you said. A little dark guy stuck his head in a couple of times, Belknap I think. I haven't seen anyone else."

"And no one else has gone up those stairs?"

Miller grinned at him. "Not since that black piece came in from outside, looking all hot and bothered."

Locken breathed heavily and dropped into a chair. The nervous energy was abandoning him. His head was light with exhaustion. From somewhere in the rear of the inn came the sound of water running.

"What's that?"

Miller jumped his shoulders nervously. "The char, probably. She was cleaning the bar just before you came in. Now what?"

Locken rubbed his eyes. "Give Nyoka and Femi a chance to rest a while longer. Then we'll move out. I don't want to . . ."

It took what seemed an eternity for Locken to recognize the sound humming in the background of his own words. An auto horn, the reedy, distinctive monotone of a London taxi wailing from the carpark.

Miller's eyes seemed to shrink. The magazine fell from his lap, the Colt revolver in the hand beneath it.

Locken was on his feet when he heard the first heavy footfalls on the stairs, descending quickly, the piercing call of the autohorn unceasing.

He spun to face the archway leading from the lounge toward the stairs, his body dropping painfully into a shooter's crouch. Mack filled the archway, face flushed red, pointing the heavy Webley pistol uncertainly.

"Mack!"

Mack blinked, bewildered in the dim light. "That's Burt. The char said you were in trouble. She said . . ."

"The char?" Locken pushed roughly forward, leaping for the stairs. He pulled himself upward, using the banister, taking them in two's and three's.

Ahead of him he could hear the rhythmic thumping. Once, again, and then again.

At the top of the stairwell he saw her, to his left. A charwoman's loose blue uniform, the mock-laced half-apron pulled too tightly across the hips, raven hair concealed beneath a floppy hat. Elise Roqué reared back and threw her weight violently against a door halfway along the hall, one hand twisting to free a key in the lock, at the end of a long, slender chain at her waist. The door was open a crack, braced from inside.

Again Elise hurled herself at the door. From behind the door Femi screamed, "Get away, you little bitch."

Elise took a step back, snapped the chain with an angry pull, her right hand reaching beneath her uniform.

"Elise!"

She stiffened like a rabbit caught in a hunter's light, then whirled to face him.

Behind him he could hear Mack and Miller pounding up the stairs. Elise remained absolutely rigid for a bare instant before the right hand came out of the uniform holding a heavy Colt automatic. It raised, raised too far, then was loose in the air, whirling end over end toward the ceiling. Elise put one foot behind the other to keep from falling, the bullet from Miller's pistol making a small dark spot on her left breast.

Miller tried to shove Locken aside, force himself past, already raising the revolver for another shot. Locken turned on him. The heavy automatic slashed down across his outstretched arm, the sick crunch of impact blending with Miller's dog-yelp of pain.

Locken brought the gun barrel down again, high on Miller's right shoulder. Miller dipped and stumbled to the floor. Locken stepped toward him to wound with his feet, fighting the arm that circled him from behind, not wanting to hear the calm voice in his ear telling him, "No more Michael, enough Michael."

Locken tore loose and turned toward Elise. When he reached her, she was still breathing, her chest fluttering rapidly trying to claw life from the air. A viscous stain spread out from beneath her.

Around him Locken was vaguely aware of the faces that emerged cautiously from each door. Of the slim, dark, frightened man assuring them there wasn't any danger, to be calm, the police were on their way.

Mack guided Femi and Nyoka past him. When he

turned to look for Miller he was no longer where he had fallen.

Locken tried to ease her back, but she grabbed at his hand, trying to pull herself up. She smiled at him, a fevered look behind her eyes; for a moment they remained sharply focused.

"You wouldn't have shot me, Miguel."

"Probably not."

"You're not so hard, like me."

"Were you the one, Elise?"

She moved her hands over his, feeling each finger separately, every configuration. "No good guys, Miguel. That's what you told me, remember. I was the one, cariño. It was always me."

She lay back then, the smile not quite leaving her lips. Locken stayed until the brightness in her eyes clouded and there was no longer strength in her hands. Then he got up slowly and walked back down the stairs.

18

THEY RODE in silence, the lengthening fingers of an orange dawn reaching across the sky behind them.

"How long will Belknap wait before he phones the police?" Locken's voice was flat, controlled.

"He said ten minutes," replied Mack, behind the wheel again.

"That's a long time with a body and nervous people."

"He's making five quid a minute. I gave him fifty."

"When the police show, he'll earn it. Belknap won't do us any favors, especially when they tell him what they found out there in the trees. There'll be law all over Cudwyp in a few hours."

"Will that matter?" said Femi acidly, her look averting his.

Moses Nyoka slumped next to her, his massive head bent, chin nearly on chest. His eyes were yellowed, staring at the empty road ahead of them.

Miller rode in front next to Mack, his face turned rigidly forward.

"It won't matter to you. You and your father will be in Amsterdam. What you do after that is your business."

Nyoka raised his head, his voice without resonance. "You speak of our rendezvous with great confidence, Mr. Locken."

"Don't let it fool you."

"The plane will come?"

"It will come."

Without further exchange they both understood it was a last slim chance. The tide was welling against them: the foul weather, the turnabout in Buwanda, the tightening of the police search, the sure presence of Hansen and Bouche. Locken had mentally added another factor: the difficulty of procuring a plane on short notice and having it arrive at the end of the bloody earth at the right moment.

"How much time do we have?" asked Mack.

"An hour, and we'll need all of it." Locken could see something stirring in Mack, beneath the surface. "Stay on this road until you see a sign that points to the Evans farm."

"At the inn, Michael . . ." Mack coughed lightly.

"Forget it. You're not the first man she's fooled."

"It was Burt's horn. It didn't seem like something they'd do. Not if they wanted to surprise us."

"That was the idea," Locken said slowly.

"Then she was knocking on the door, saying 'Mr. Locken sent me, Mr. Locken is in trouble.' And me looking out and seeing nothing but a tatty old char, and not even her very well." He stopped, buffered by his own reference to his eyes. "I didn't think." He smiled vacantly at the admission. The thought that he had lost his usual calm under stress seemed to have stunned him, as it had Locken.

Since he had seen the shocked look of bewilderment on Mack's face in the lounge, an ugly little animal had been burrowing away in Locken's abdomen, tossing up at him Cap Collis's warning about Mack's talents for their business fading with age. It was running closer to prophecy than Locken wanted to admit. First his eyes, then the indecision. The thought left Locken with a sick emptiness, worsened because he knew he was unable to prevent Mack from unleashing on himself an uncompromising, harsh self-criticism.

"It was nobody's fault," said Locken.

Mack gave his impatient snort, staring ahead.

Femi looked at him questioningly. "But why go to the trouble? What was she going to do?"

"I'm not sure," Locken replied. "Whatever she was trying, she couldn't risk it while someone was guarding you. She might have been trying to let you know she was going to help. Or maybe fake an attempt so the others wouldn't suspect her."

"Or kill the old boy," said Miller without turning. "You thought of that, didn't you, Mr. Locken?"

"I thought of it, Miller. I know that pistol didn't come out until she began to lose control of the situation. And I know, at least I think I know, what she tried to tell me before she died."

"You guess she was the double?" asked Mack.

"We better assume so until either Bouche or Hansen brings us a bouquet of apology."

"Anything you say, Mr. Locken," said Miller.

Locken ignored his obvious sarcasm. He couldn't expect better. Miller had followed orders, reacted quickly, and shot fast. Locken had pistol-whipped him for it, and would have done worse if Mack hadn't pulled him away. In his place Locken wouldn't have continued a minute, not with a professional who had lost the essential ingredient, self-control.

Locken addressed Miller evenly, with some effort. "Is your arm all right?"

"It's fine."

"You're sure?"

"I said it's okay." Miller squeezed his right fist tentatively.

"Michael?" Mack nodded toward a white pole with a single pointer, the name Evans lettered on it in square black letters.

"That's it," said Locken, thankful for the distraction. "Go right."

Mack spun the wheel, taking Burt along a narrow dirt road.

As they made the turn Locken glanced back. A mile or so behind them he thought he saw an automobile, but in the half-light he couldn't be sure.

A moment later Mack said, "Evans place. Dead ahead."

Parallel to the dirt road ran a 3-foot-high stake fence, and beyond it Locken saw the familiar small white two-storied house with carefully painted green trimming, a little too precisely drawn. A light was on in the kitchen; smoke curled from a chimney.

"Cozy," said Mack, with a curiously constricted undertone.

Past the house, across the farmyard, Locken could clearly make out the string of lights brightly illuminating the interior of a modern, tin-roofed, milking barn. From the barn came the unmistakable bleating of dairy cows awaiting their morning milking. A staid royal-blue Humber sedan was parked close to the house.

Mack slowed Burt to ease over an old wooden bridge, the clear, swift-flowing water of a small stream surging beneath it. Locken pointed to a tire track leading off into thick brush, just ahead.

"Turn in and keep going."

Mack down-shifted into first gear, guiding the front wheels into deep parallel tracks. Immediately they were again enveloped in darkness.

Heavy undergrowth brushed the sides of the taxi and wiry trees grew up on either side to interlock in a dense canopy of foliage above them.

Mack switched on the spotlights, his eyes meeting Locken's in the rearview mirror. "Maybe you better tell us what happens now, Michael." The prod was gentle but firm.

Locken nodded, his neck muscles sore, his head heavy with fatigue. He pushed the tiredness from his voice. "The Evans place back there is at the wide end of a valley, almost three miles long. We're in it now. We'll be able to take this track about another mile, to a clearing the locals come to for firewood."

"What then?"

Locken understood that Mack's questioning was done for the others as well. They had come this far on faith; it would carry them no farther.

"At the clearing we'll have to leave Burt and go on foot. A path leads another half mile to the longhouse of an old farm. Below it is the pasture where the plane will land."

"And after that?"

"We deal with Hansen and Bouche and whoever they brought to the party."

"They'll never follow us in here," said Miller. He slipped off his glasses, breathed on them, and rubbed with a soft cloth. "They for sure know we've been using that beeper to bait them."

Mack raised his eyebrows. "He's right, Michael. Suppose they don't accept the invitation?"

"They'll come."

Femi turned, startled at the sureness in his voice. "Because they want my father?"

"That. And because until now we've beaten them. Hansen has never been beaten. God knows about Bouche. My guess is nothing will shake him loose. I've seen his kind of fanatic pursuit. A Nazi hunter we once took out from the East, a wiry little Hungarian Jew, showed me how deep an obsession can go. Bouche won't give up now until he kills us or we kill him."

"What if they catch up before our guest here departs?" asked Mack.

"We have to make sure they don't. We've got a lead on them. Once we're on foot they'll have to feel their way along or risk being ambushed." Locken looked at the old man and Femi. "You'll be safe in Amsterdam before anything happens." Nyoka didn't appear to hear him.

"Is this the only way into the valley?" Locken felt an attentiveness in Miller that surprised him.

"By car it's the only way."

"Only way in, means the only way out," said Mack, a little forlornly.

"Patience, Mr. MacKinney. I'm coming to that. Beyond the pasture where the plane will land, the valley begins to narrow. A mile on, it pinches together and appears to dead-end."

"Oh, my," said Mack.

"Only it doesn't. That stream we crossed runs the length of the valley and cuts through a narrow pass at the far end, about a half-mile long."

"Where does the pass go?" asked Miller.

"Back to Cudwyp."

Miller's prim mouth warped in thought. He grinned and asked, "How do you want to play it, Mr. Locken?" His tone was scornful.

Locken let it go. "Depends on two things. The time we have. And how many of them come for us. I'd like to set an ambush. The only way to move along that valley is via the path, or the bed of the stream."

"And saying we don't have time?"

"Wait until we make contact, and let them push us along the valley. If they come from this direction it will seem a natural retreat. A couple of hundred yards short of that pass, the geology has fits. There are some ancient terraces thirty or forty feet above the valley floor that you can't see until you're on top of them. We can take them from there. I'd like to get Hansen alive. If possible," he added.

Miller's voice was an incredulous whine. "You think they'll walk into a trap like that?"

"I don't think they'll walk into anything. They'll play this out because they want us. If we look like we're running scared their blood is liable to get up enough for them to keep chasing until they catch us. Don't forget it's going to look like our back is against the wall, and a little adrenalin in the blood doesn't make you see things any straighter."

Mack's eyes snapped to the rearview, and too late Locken realized that Mack had taken it as criticism of his actions at the inn. "What if they're more cautious than I was, Michael?"

"If we get in a jam we'll take the easy way out. Straight through the pass back to Cudwyp. That pass is our safety valve."

"What if the plane don't come?" asked Miller.

Nyoka blinked once slowly. Femi looked at Miller with a mixture of disbelief and loathing.

"We play it the same way. Through the pass to Cud-wyp."

Femi spoke to Locken, her voice no longer challenging in her need for reassurance. "But you said the plane would come."

Locken began nodding. "That's what I said all right."

The tire track widened suddenly into a large clearing several hundred feet across, dotted with stumps and fallen trees.

"This is as far as we can drive, Mack. We'll have to walk the rest of the way."

Mack made a full U-turn until Burt was pointed back the direction they had come before stopping. He sat motionless behind the wheel while the others got out.

Nyoka accepted Femi's helping hand from the taxi without resisting. The girl carried the green canvas bag she had brought from her apartment. Miller hoisted his valise from the floor of the taxi and stepped down, taking in his surroundings with an uncomfortable glance. He worked his fist several times and lifted out the carbine.

"While you're at it, Miller, let's have a look in the valise."

Miller drew the bag close to him. "What for?"

"Another beeper. We found one. We might not have found them all. From here on we can't afford too close a tag."

"Yeah, sure." Miller stuck his face in the valise and looked up grinning. "I'm clean. What about her?" He nodded toward Femi's bag.

"Sorry, Femi."

She held out the bag. "Not much left to dig through is there, Locken?"

"I just work here." He emptied the small plastic zipper bag brimming with her makeup, and pressed through the items of clothing he had watched her hastily pack only twelve hours before. It seemed longer; stress had its own way with time. When he was satisfied she carried nothing electronic, he looked toward the others. "All right, let's go."

He led them rapidly along the path, away from the clearing, deeper into the valley. The rush of the swiftly flowing stream a few yards to their right absorbed all other noises, including, Locken knew, the sound of any vehicle that might have followed them along the tire track.

Twenty minutes later, the path widened onto a grassy patch cleared of brush and trees. Ahead of them, some fifty yards, was the longhouse of the old farm, built of flat slabs of gray stone and settled on its foundation until not a right angle remained anywhere in its construction. Locken grinned at Mack. "You'll look that way too when you're nine hundred years old."

"Michael, I feel like I look that way right now."

Miller paused for a moment, craning his head around in slow sweep, almost as though he were sniffing the air with his small perfect nose. Checking fields of fire, Locken guessed. He had done the same thing months before. The longhouse could be defended, if it came to that.

Locken stopped and pointed. Slightly below them in elevation still several hundred yards distant was the pasture. Roughly rectangular in shape, surface of tufted grass, visibly uneven.

"Where's this pass you were talking about?" said Miller.

"Only one place it could be, Miller. Look along the valley there about a mile."

"It just sort of appears to end."

"That's where the pass begins. It's about twenty, thirty feet wide at best. The stream cuts right through it with a

trail running straight along the bank. The longhouse here
is almost midpoint in the valley."

"And the plane's going to land there?" said Miller
pointing toward the pasture, his inflection rising in disbelief.

"Right there." Something in Locken's voice made
Miller look at him again and shuffle away.

Locken glanced at his watch. The aircraft was due in
seven minutes. The anxiety began to squeeze a renewed
alertness into his body. "Come on. It's nearly time."

He led them back onto the path toward the pasture.
Behind him he could hear Moses Nyoka breathing heavily
in the crisp morning air.

19

"I SAW SOMETHING, I'm tell-
ing you." Miller's eyes were hidden behind the glasses.

The aircraft was already six minutes overdue. When
they reached the edge of the pasture Locken had sent
Miller back along the path to a point high enough to
cover them and watch the grassy space near the longhouse.

Nyoka had hunkered down, back to a tree trunk, the
lines of tiredness along the sides of his broad nose like
creases in dark leather. His eyes hadn't joined Mack's and
Femi's in their slow sweep of horizon.

Then suddenly Miller was back, the pronouncement
clipped through grainy teeth.

Locken wanted to say impossible, but cut the word off.
"Where exactly, Miller?"

"That way." He flung his slender arm toward a point
where the valley wall began to narrow, beyond the pasture
toward the pass.

"What was it, Jerome?" Mack questioned softly, as
though trying to coax a skittish animal.

"I don't know. Something flashing, quick, two or three
times. Like sunlight reflecting off glass. Binoculars or
something."

Locken studied the landscape in the direction Miller
pointed and saw nothing.

"What do you make of it?" asked Mack.

"I swear I saw something."

"No doubt," said Locken. "The question is, What?"

Mack squinted thoughtfully: "Could someone have come through that pass from Cudwyp side?"

"Our friends? Possible. They'd have needed the right kind of receiver to track the beeper, and a large-scale map of the area to do it." Locken frowned toward the pass. "That's stacking a lot of ifs together."

"Risk it if you want, Mr. Locken. But if it's them, they sure got us in a neat trap."

"Trap?" Femi studied Miller's face, as if searching for another meaning of the word.

"We don't know what Miller saw. Nobody's trapped."

"But if the plane doesn't come,'" Femi began. Locken reached around and grabbed her by the arm.

"That aircraft is late, that's all. This is rough country."

"You're right, of course," she replied quickly, looking at her father.

Mack squatted on his heels, and cleared a space on the ground with his hand, drawing with a twig as he spoke. "Michael, I'm no pilot, but I've been doing some reckoning. Considering the orientation of this valley, any pilot that wants to get a decent crack at setting down on this pasture has got to come in close to where Miller said he saw that reflection."

"I did see it."

"All right, Jerome." Mack made no effort to conceal his exasperation. "If Hansen or one of them did manage to come through that pass, he's more than a stopper in the bottle. He'll be close enough to take a crack at that plane before it can land."

"Or when it takes off." Locken scooped a fistful of dirt and ground it around between his fingers. "Okay, Miller.

Work your way around the pasture. Pick up the path on the other side and follow it to where you saw the reflection. And keep your eyes open."

Miller grinned, a tip of tongue moving along small teeth. "What if nothing happens?"

"Consider yourself a lucky man," said Mack.

"If trouble arrives before the aircraft"—Locken hesitated, reluctant to admit that now, perhaps, they had no safety valve left—"we'll fall back on the longhouse."

"Got it," said Miller, moving off in a half-run, carrying his valise under his left arm protectively.

"Do you suppose Miller had parents," said Mack, watching him go. "Or if one day he came out from under a rock, guns and all."

"It does make a man wonder."

Five minutes more on Locken's watch; it felt like fifty. He sent Mack back along the path to check the grassy space near the longhouse and saw him return shaking his head. Femi watched the sky. Nyoka's yellowed eyes looked ahead, seeing nothing.

Locken looked at them both, knowing at some point he had to admit the plane wasn't coming, that something had gone wrong. Blame Collis, blame Willie something-or-other, blame the pilot or himself or a carburetor, or a clerk who had to approve a flight plan. Blame somebody, admit it, then get ready. Only Hansen and Bouche would come, if they hadn't already. The margin of lead-time was gone.

Locken started to speak when Femi looked up, cocking her head. A faint smile played across her lips, her eyes widening.

"I hear it."

Locken turned his head back and forth, listening. He

heard nothing. He saw Moses Nyoka shake his head con-
firming the silence.

The aircraft rose suddenly over the end of the valley,
the high-pitched buzz of its engine reaching them a moment later.

Single-engined, with high, thick wings, their trailing
edges elongated by enormous flaps. The abnormally wide
wing-span made it look like a drab metal dragonfly. A
British design, its make unfamiliar to Locken, but the
distinctive silhouette unmistakably intended for short
takeoffs and landings.

The pitch of the engine dropped slightly and the aircraft floated down toward the floor of the valley, the tips
of the broad wings appearing to almost touch the valley
walls. With less than fifty feet of altitude the plane
straightened and flew toward them, head on, its wings
waggling slightly as the pilot delicately maneuvered the
plane still closer to the treetops along the valley floor.

"That's a bit of flying," said Mack, in open admiration.

Locken grunted tightly and stepped forward into the
pasture. He waved his arm over his head.

Moses Nyoka rose slowly, brushed leaves from his
trousers, one huge hand pulling at the collar of his shirt
and straightening his necktie.

His momentary surprise gone, Locken now watched
transfixed. Landing speed looked to be something less
than forty miles per hour; in its unbelievably slow approach the aircraft appeared to defy principles of flight.

Over the edge of the pasture it dropped until the spindly
landing gear almost touched the ground. Then a rising
buzz and the plane lifted.

"It's not going to land," Femi shouted above the sound
of the engine.

"Not this time," said Locken. "He'll fly over it and have
a look at the landing surface. Next time around."

A hundred feet from them, the pilot gunned the engine, pulling up sharply to clear the trees at the edge of the pasture.

As the aircraft passed directly overhead Locken could see the pilot clearly. Hard flight helmet, the dark lenses of flying glasses, and beneath, incongruously, a flowing white walrus moustache on a jowly face.

The pilot gave a jaunty "thumbs up" and banked away, climbing for altitude, rising up over the valley wall.

Locken turned to Nyoka. "It's okay. Next time he'll land." He realized his hand was resting lightly on the butt of his automatic.

With the plane gone the silence was on them again, this time charged with energy. Femi stifled a grin. Even Mack couldn't contain a lean smile. Nyoka stood stiffly, waiting.

A moment later the aircraft appeared almost in the exact spot they had first seen it. The pilot neatly slipped it over the valley wall, bringing it into a low flat approach, still a quarter of a mile from the pasture.

"Christ," said Locken.

"Will you look at that," Mack said, awed at the pilot's skill.

The long-winged aircraft was dropping gracefully, Locken's jaw taut at the agonizing slowness of its approach, when, still fifty yards short of the pasture, he heard the engine backfire.

Next to him, Mack bent forward, his eyes, Locken knew, intuitively looking for the telltale puff of blue exhaust that accompanied cylinder misfire. There was none. Locken heard the pop again, recognizing it this time for what it was. A gunshot, barely distinguishable as separate from engine noise.

"They're shooting at it," yelled Femi, the disbelief turning to helplessness. "They're shooting . . ."

Locken's eyes riveted on the frail aircraft, hoping

against reason that the bullets had left it and its pilot untouched. For a few long seconds it looked as though, impossibly, it was so, as the aircraft continued its precise course toward them without change.

Then slowly, as if part of some preplanned aerobatics, the right wing tip began to rise. Still in what appeared perfect control, the aircraft rotated a full ninety degrees on its axis of flight, until the left wing tip now pointed directly toward the ground, the other skyward.

For scant seconds the aircraft maintained an impossible attitude, still graceful in flight. Then the left wing tip brushed earth, and it was jerked from the sky. The aircraft cartwheeled angrily, engine screaming out of control, and exploded, orange flames mushrooming until they swallowed the entire wreckage.

They stood, frozen in unbelieving silence. Broken then by the distinctive sound of Miller's carbine in the direction of the pass, firing rapidly.

20

RUNNING, they had nearly reached the longhouse when off to their left, through the trees, came the dull crump of a plastic charge, the muffled explosion like a firecracker in a rain barrel, unmistakable.

The sound brought Mack up as though he had been struck. "Burt!" Locken pushed him forward. His head lowered, they began again to run.

Across the door of the longhouse a bar of mild steel was padlocked over a heavy hasp. The windows, Locken knew, were securely shuttered with inch thick oak planking, bolted in place from inside, backed by heavy-gauge wire mesh.

He shot the lock off without hesitation and stepped into the dim interior. A wave of damp, fetid air met him. If failure had a smell, to Locken that was it.

He moved through the rooms in quick strides, searching for anything amiss. Half of the house had once been an interior barn, where generations of inhabitants had lived under the same roof with their animals as equal members of the family. In the bedroom his eyes rested an instant on the light-cord, severed a few inches from the ceiling when he had cut down Gunter Rachman. There had never been a telephone. He spun stiffly and went back to the others.

Without a word he and Mack pulled loose the shutters from the two windows.

One looked across fifty yards of open grass toward the path leading back to the clearing where they had left Burt. A long half mile now, thought Locken. Evans's farm was another mile beyond that.

The second window covered the uphill approach from the pasture, the wreckage of the aircraft still burning fiercely. A mile on the other side, the narrowing of the valley walls marked the pass to Cudwyp. They had finished when Miller came into view, running flat-out toward the longhouse, the short carbine cradled in the crook of an arm, the valise swinging.

"It was Hansen," he explained out of breath, feeding stubby brass cartridges into the magazine. "I didn't see him till he shot the pilot." He looked at Locken and grinned. "Cripes, I could have hit that old boy with a rock, the speed he was flying."

"What happened to Hansen?"

"I shot at him, but I was just shooting at bushes." Miller looked around again. "He just sort of disappeared."

Locken listened, reluctant to believe Hansen had done it. Now he was waiting somewhere in the mile between the longhouse and the narrow pass out of the valley that meant safety.

"We are trapped, aren't we, Mr. Locken?" said Femi.

"Where he is, Hansen is like an anvil. It depends on how Bouche intends to swing the hammer."

"Bouche?" said Miller.

"Coming up from the pasture we heard an explosion. Bouche got to Burt."

Miller paled. "They're out there." He gestured in the direction of Evans's farm with his carbine.

"Why should that be such a surprise?"

"If they were there, why not keep coming, is all. Before we were ready."

"I don't know. That's why I want to find out what Bouche is up to."

"I prefer not to wait," said Nyoka. He was on his feet, the yellow gone from his eyes. His chest despite the run was scarcely heaving.

"What do you suggest?"

"Take the initiative. We mustn't wait."

Locken studied him a moment. It was as if the shock of seeing his last chance destroyed had broken through to some reserve of energy. The malaise was gone.

"It's not our choice."

Nyoka paused. "Perhaps not. But if I'm to die, it will not be waiting calmly in a pen built for animals. That choice, Mr. Locken, remains mine."

"You're not going to die," said Femi, partly in anger, partly in self-assurance.

Locken said, "We can defend this house indefinitely if we have to."

"Against explosives?" Nyoka's loud guffaw told him how badly he had lied. The old man began pacing, his face immobile in thought.

Locken smiled, forced to admire Nyoka's not-give-a-damn resilience. He turned to Mack, who had posted himself silently at one of the windows, the Webley resting on the ledge.

"Wake up, Mr. MacKinney. You are about to assume command of the fort."

For once Mack was without a ready answer. He stared at Locken blankly, then appeared to understand.

"What are you going to do?" asked Femi, a hint of alarm in her voice.

"We know where Hansen is. Bouche is the question

mark. I'm going to push in his direction until I get some shove. To Evans's farm if I have to." Nyoka stopped pacing when Locken addressed him. "If we can find a hole to slip through in either direction you might stand a chance of going home yet. A gnat-sized one."

"It's not for myself, Mr. Locken."

"I know that." He later remembered how easily the words had come.

Nyoka laughed, almost brightly. "For myself I wish only a less shameful end."

"Stop it!" said Femi.

Mack stepped forward. "I'll come along, Michael. See what they done to Burt."

Locken shook his head. "I'll find out, Mack. I need you here." Their eyes met, but Mack's dropped away. "Stay close to the radio."

Miller was grinning again. "This was some idea you had, Mr. Locken."

Locken grinned back. "Come on, Miller."

"What for?"

"I've got a job for you."

"Up there will do." Locken indicated a gray boulder the size of Burt, almost hidden by a stand of stunted Corsican pine growing thickly around its base.

From the top of the boulder Locken judged Miller could cover both the path that led back to the clearing and Evans's farm, and the stream channel. The longhouse was close enough at his back to retreat if trouble came.

Miller moved his head around uneasily. "Why don't I stay inside? At least I got some protection inside."

"Ah, Miller, I can tell you're a city boy."

Miller pushed the glasses back on his nose. "I'll bet Hansen can move through this country like an Indian, that's what I bet." He added, almost as an afterthought. "I seen him do it."

"Between the longhouse and the pass he's dangerous. Why should he wander?"

"The house would be safer, is all." Miller's voice had its perpetual whine.

"Unless Bouche gets close to it with a few kilos of plastic. That's why you're out here." It wasn't the entire reason; but it was enough.

Locken handed him the other radio. "If you get lonely, call Mack. He'll cheer you up."

"I'm not scared, Mr. Locken. Don't think that."

"I don't think anything." Locken left him, hunched down next to the boulder, the carbine clutched tightly in his small, delicate hands.

Moving with any speed or stealth through the dense undergrowth Locken knew would be impossible. Of the two choices remaining, the path or the stream, he chose the latter.

The moment he stepped into the swiftly flowing current, going in to his knees, the sharp, numbing spikes of cold drove upward along his legs. He went forward, dragging his feet along the graveled bottom, rather than risk that the sound of his feet, breaking the surface with each step, might carry.

Staying close to the bank he moved quickly, until he came to the first of what would be a dozen or so, low, fast-flowing waterfalls, several feet high. At each, Locken left the stream, reentering it again above the obstacle. In those moments he felt totally naked.

If Bouche was ahead of him he was hoping for some warning, however slight. If others were with him, perhaps muffled voices, the smell of cigarettes.

After twenty minutes, nothing. Only once did he hear any sound discordant against the unvarying tone of flowing water. Ahead, out of sight above the next fall, he heard what might have been a stone clattering against another, a distinctive resonant clack. He stopped, pistol raised, counting seconds until they became minutes. He saw nothing, heard nothing human, then went on.

He stopped a few minutes later when he smelt burnt rubber. To his right the air had an oily blue haze. He climbed from the stream bed cautiously, moving at right angles to it, until he came to the edge of the clearing. There was no need to go farther. He could see Burt; the damage done to the taxi was enough. It occurred to him that a few sharp hammer blows would have done the job; it was as though Bouche had focused his anger on the taxi. Burt's hood was peeled open, radiator blown forward, the entire front end gaping at him like a raw wound.

He returned to the stream. It took him the better part of an hour before he lay prone, looking beyond the wooden bridge toward Evans's farm. The puzzlement long since had given way to a low alarm of warning.

Locken took a full minute to study each of the three buildings. The small, prim house closest to the road. Diagonally across the farm yard, the milking barn. And next to it, nearest the cover of trees, a large, older building with a rounded roof—a utility barn, Locken guessed.

Nothing had changed in the slightest. The same staid Humber sedan; the same curl of smoke from the chimney; the cry of cattle from the milking barn, and still no one in sight. The sameness of it probed beneath Locken's consciousness like a splinter and stayed there to fester. "Peaceful," he said under his breath. "Very peaceful."

Even as he said it, the back door of the house opened

and a man stepped onto the porch. At a distance of more than a hundred yards Locken could see little. A small man of indeterminate middle age, dressed in rough clothing. He made a steeple of fingers, pressing both hands together in a lazy stretch, and began a leisurely walk across the farmyard toward the utility barn.

Locken made up his mind. Using ferns, then low brush, he skirted the periphery of the farmyard toward the utility barn, unseen by anyone in the house had they been looking, he was sure.

In the trees twenty feet or so from the entrance he stopped. The interior of the barn was unlit. He could see nothing.

Locken pushed the automatic into his belt, stepped from cover, and walked to the open door feeling as nonchalant as a chicken thief.

He was nearly there when the man came through it, brushing flecks of hay from his baggy tweed trousers.

He stopped almost in mid-step when he saw Locken, his face stretching long with surprise.

The gun was in Locken's hand again, brought up to arm's length and sighted in one motion. "Right there will do."

"What do you want?"

The man's voice was tinged with an impatience that made Locken, wet to the knees, unshaven, gun in hand, feel more than slightly ridiculous.

The man went back to brushing the hay from his faded plaid shirt, which was open at the collar, touching once the row of pens and paraphernalia lining his breast pocket, arranged neatly in a white plastic liner.

Close up, the man was more compactly put together than he had looked from a distance. Thick neck, small wide hands, with sinewy forearms. Hair thinning. A face hardly memorable, but curiously composed.

"Who are you?" said Locken.

"Evans. Who did you expect?"

His voice had a forced guttural quality, provoked by what might have been a typical Welsh reluctance to speak English.

"Hope you can prove it."

"I don't have to prove it. You're on my property."

His crustiness, even at gun point, made Locken smile. "Okay, Mr. Evans. I was looking for you."

"You found me." He dropped his eyes to the pistol in Locken's hand. "What do you want with me?"

"What have you seen in the past few hours?"

"Nothing worth telling. I've been in there." He tossed a thumb toward the milking barn.

"Your wife?"

"She's at market, if it's business of yours?"

"It's my business. Take my word on it. You have a phone?"

Evans nodded, running his finger tips absently along the row of pens.

"I'd like to call the police."

"With my pleasure," he said quickly, still watching the pistol. He gestured toward the house. "It's in the kitchen."

"After you."

"Do you want my hands up?"

"Not unless you're comfortable that way."

Locken followed him toward the house, leaving a full two yards between them. Through the door of the milking barn black-and-white faces turned toward him in unison only to bend back against metal stays and give him a discordant bleat.

The kitchen was warm and comfortable, the principal source of both, a cast-iron, wood-burning stove, set conspicuously next to a modern, white-enameled electric cooker. A large kettle steamed at the back. A square oak table in the center of the kitchen still had dishes on it from breakfast.

"I'll make tea." Evans made an attempt at a friendly smile, and began pawing through dirty dishes in the sink. "The phone's on the wall behind you."

Locken backed toward it, his eyes curious, watching Evans's benign, not unpleasant profile.

Evans found the teapot, rinsed it slowly, and turned unhurriedly toward the stove.

Locken shifted the pistol to his right hand and reached around for the phone. He lifted it from the cradle, wondering if he could hear above the bleat of cattle, penetrating even at a distance. There was nothing to hear. The phone was dead. Dirty dishes, bleating cattle, the same placid face watching him from the back of the orange-and-white van leaving an African Airways DC-8.

"Cream and sugar, Bouche, if you have any."

The steaming kettle was already in the air, spewing scalding water as it wobbled elliptically toward him. Locken ducked, trying at the same time to shift his pistol from right hand to left. The kettle struck the wall above him, showering his back with fire.

Bouche sprang forward against the table, pushing it toward Locken with his weight behind it. The edge of the table caught him groin high, slamming Locken back to the wall with a grunt of expelled breath.

Locken jerked his wrist free, the automatic thrust toward Bouche's chest a table width away. Already the length of wire stretched between Bouche's clenched fists, taut and shiny. He stepped quickly sidewise, using the garrot as a policeman might fend off a blow with a baton, parrying the outstretched muzzle of the automatic away from him. The wire looped Locken's wrist. There was a blinding shot of pain, a scream Locken realized was his own, as the pistol was wrenched from his grip.

Locken made a groping stab for Bouche's throat with his unbending right arm, pushing at the same time with his buttocks against the wall behind him for leverage. Bouche pulled at the table, leaving Locken for a fraction of a second without resistance and off balance. Before he could recover, Bouche reached forward. There was a razor slice across Locken's throat as the garrot tightened, Bouche's face red with focused energy, an angry hum escaping his lips.

Locken's eyes were trying to roll from his head, fingers no longer reaching for the knife at his ankle but clawing at his own throat, tearing at the wire about to sever his head cleanly from his body. Locken's right fist grabbed for nothing, then followed the elbow downward in a rapid arc. He felt his elbow sink in, and for a bare instant the garrot loosened. Locken used it to turn, striking with stiffened fingers at the openness of an armpit. A sharp cry and the garrot whirled loose from one fist. Then Locken was behind him, his left arm locked around Bouche's midsection. With one foot against the wall, Locken catapulted them both forward, clasped together like lovers, Bouche's foot catching, their bodies falling, only to strike the hard, metal edge of the cooker.

The explosion was little more than a muffled crack totally without resonance. Locken felt Bouche lift beneath him, the mild grunt, as though a powerful fist had driven out his breath. The acrid smell of fulminate filled Locken's nostrils. Then nothing. Bouche lay still.

Locken rolled away, and lay on the floor until he thought he could move. He pulled himself upright, touching the motionless Bouche on the shoulder. He turned him over. The left side of his chest was a sticky pulp.

In the wound, Locken could see bits of metal. Bouche had carried more than pens and pencils in his breast pocket. A percussion detonator perhaps. Even the pencil fuses Bouche would have used with gelignite Locken knew were powerful and fast. Any detonator would fire under a sharp blow. Whatever they were had pulverized Bouche's heart, in a fraction of a second measured in thousandths.

Locken stood, found his pistol, waited until his thighs stopped shaking, then walked across the farmyard. He paused long enough in the milking barn to turn the cattle loose; their mournful cry would continue until someone relieved their pain, udders swollen and full, long past the time that Evans would have milked them that morning.

In the utility barn he dug into the hay until he uncovered the soles of two sets of shoes, one men's, the other no doubt Mrs. Evans's. He went no farther.

Locken stood, knowing he couldn't afford more time. Yet the separate facts were still patterning themselves in his mind. Bouche hadn't pursued them after destroying Burt because he'd been alone. He'd known about the telephone because he'd used it before cutting the line. And whatever came next would benefit from an absence of witnesses.

As Locken wondered how much time he would have, the crunch of automobile tires sliding to a stop in the farmyard gave him an answer: no time at all.

He stepped quickly back from the door, moving sidewise in the half darkness, until he could see out.

A black, muddied Jaguar 420 Saloon had stopped behind the Humber. And behind it the gray Rover. In two cars Locken counted seven men. The car doors opened in unison.

Locken waited long enough to see the first man step from the Jaguar. In his left hand he held what appeared to be two feet of water pipe, with a 30-round clip. The unmistakable, deadly functional shape of a Sten machine pistol.

21

NYOKA'S MOUTH curved down
into a stiff, inverted crescent when Locken explained
what had happened at Evans's farm.

In the half hour it had taken him to return to the
longhouse the day had turned overcast. The dampness
clung to him, the air in the longhouse scarcely warming.

"They arrived very quickly, Mr. Locken," Nyoka
commented without lightness.

"My guess is they didn't have far to come. Bouche or
Hansen could have called for reinforcements last night.
To London most likely. By the time they set off tracking
us this morning the hired help might not have arrived.
They probably picked some point near Cudwyp as a
rendezvous. All Bouche had to do was call them from
wherever they caught up with us."

"Not me," whined Miller. "Not against seven guys with
Stens."

"What now, Mr. Locken?" Nyoka's tone signaled
readiness to reject any answer which failed to suit him.

"We can't wait to see how long it takes those gunmen
to come this far."

"Or?"

"Or we can try for Cudwyp on foot."

Mack moved his bony shoulders in a careless shrug.

Miller bent close to the carbine, working the action, apparently oblivious of all else.

"Do you think Hansen is still waiting?" asked Femi, shivering visibly in the cold.

"He's had no reason to change his mind. It's a good mile between here and the pass, and rough country all the way. He could be anywhere."

"Then I think it's time we dealt with Mr. Hansen."

Nyoka pulled the necktie from around his thick neck. He slipped off his jacket and began unbuttoning his white shirt.

"Don't be silly," said Femi.

The sudden tension beneath her words gave Locken a cue. He looked at the old man, understanding. "No. Hansen is mine."

"And apparently more than a match, Mr. Locken. He may be yours, but he is waiting for me." He peeled off his shirt. Beneath it he wore a vest of netted, thermal underwear, its narrow straps cutting into the softness over his still-heavily-muscled shoulders. "I intend to remain his prey not one second longer."

Locken spoke rapidly. "The four of you can follow the stream. The banks are several feet high, which will give you better protection than the path. It runs to the pass, and after that it's less than half a mile."

"Do you suppose the fact has eluded your Mr. Hansen?" Nyoka pulled off one huge black shoe, and tossed it aside.

"He'll have to cover the stream and the path. He'll be someplace where he can see both. I'll be ahead of you looking for that someplace."

"You've said the terrain is difficult, at best. What chance will you have of finding Hansen before he sees you? One in ten? One in twenty? And if he deals with you, what then?" He stole a glance at Femi. "All of us, one by one."

"If we leave here, there's no other way."

Nyoka removed the other shoe, and made a low sigh of satisfaction. Without socks his huge feet were scarred and leathery.

"But there is another way, Mr. Locken. The two of us."

Miller looked up. "You're an old man."

It produced a broad smile. "In my country sure proof of wisdom and cunning. I assure you the bush and I are not strangers."

He stood to full height and lifted one of the cushions from the battered couch. From beneath it he took a brush knife, its broad two-foot blade rusted except for the newly honed edge.

"Now where'd he find that?" Mack said, in frank amazement.

"A closet in the kitchen contained a few gardening tools, this among them. Sheffield steel of quite good quality, actually."

"Not good enough to match a .458 bullet," said Locken.

"In such country a better weapon than you might expect." A self-conscious smile crept across Nyoka's face. "I'm afraid my daughter considers my early manhood barbaric."

Femi Nyoka looked at Locken. "You're not going to let him do it?"

Nyoka stepped forward. "Mr. Locken cannot stop me. I have been hunted. I have cowered like *fisi*, the hyena, running with my head low. I am not a child, Femi. I am a man, and I know exactly what I value." He eyed the girl with unembarrassed tenderness, then thrust his jaw toward Locken. "Whatever chance we have together, alone you have half."

"Look, Moses, I may be wrong about Hansen. He might not be out there at all."

Miller started to speak, then looked again at his carbine. Nyoka said, "But Mr. Miller saw him. And you yourself provided us very convincing logic on why he should be between the longhouse and the pass."

"That's the point. It's my logic, not Hansen's. I'm not sure what he'll try. That's why it's better if you stick close to Mack and Miller. Sort of the convoy system."

"They must protect my girl." It wasn't quite a threat.

"We can't all go on a hunt. If he decides to lie doggo to ambush us, we could have a dozen men and still might not find him. He's a trained stalker, a professional hunter, and that country must feel like home to him."

"As it does to me," said Nyoka. "You're wasting your time, Mr. Locken."

"It could all be a waste of time. We might walk straight from here to Cudwyp, and the faster we move the better. Stay with the others, Moses."

Nyoka's head shook a denial. "If Mr. Hansen is not to be found, then an old man again taking up the knife is merely an obvious symbolic gesture." He smiled. "They're sometimes most satisfying."

Locken glanced at Mack for support, but got only a helpless twitch of a grin. The brush knife twisted in Nyoka's restless hands. Locken glared at the old man a full minute, then gave Miller an angry command.

"Give him your shotgun."

"What?"

"You heard the man, Jerome," said Mack. "A dead eye like you don't need a toy like that."

Miller started to whine, but Locken, through explaining, stepped toward the valise. Miller covered it with a hand. "Okay." His eyes slid from Locken to the others with open animosity. He lifted out the shotgun delicately and handed it to Nyoka.

"You know how to use it?" asked Locken.

"I'm acquainted with such pieces." Nyoka ejected the five shells in the magazine rapidly, then fed them in again, his huge hands dominating the weapon completely. He stuffed a handful of shells into the pocket of his trousers. He looked up and nodded, satisfied. "I suggest we get on with it."

Where the vegetation thickened beyond the pasture, Locken and Nyoka went ahead of the others. None had looked at the blackened debris of the aircraft still smoldering nearby, a few slender members of air frame seeming to beckon skyward.

The valley began to narrow there, its sides riding from the stream bed through ferns, low brush, then thicker stands of pine, spruce, and birch. The path paralleled the stream a dozen yards to its left, almost impassable at points where undergrowth had reclaimed it.

"We have a mile of this stuff before the pass. We'll have to separate," said Locken. "I'll work right of the stream, you left of the path. Look for any place that might give him some height—a tree, rock ledges, anything. If you hear shooting, stay put."

Beside him, Nyoka nodded. Along with his shirt and shoes he might have left twenty years behind. His eyes alertly studied the brush ahead of them, his grip firm on the long knife.

"You mentioned terraces?"

"They're farther on, just short of the pass. They're nothing more than ledges forty or fifty feet above the

valley floor, cut when the stream flowed up there a couple
of million years ago instead of here. If I were Hansen
that's where I'd be."

"And for that reason perhaps he'll wait elsewhere."

"Perhaps."

They parted without another word. Too late, Locken
thought to give Nyoka one of the radios. He turned, but
already the huge black man had disappeared into the
brush.

Another thought occurred to Locken only moments
later: that he had chosen a very complex way to commit
suicide. His line of sight was limited to no more than a
few feet. The brush dampened the sound of the stream,
somehow exaggerating his own clumsy efforts to advance
silently. Brush closed in behind him, shielding Miller,
Mack, and Femi from his view. He swore quietly. Brush
was Hansen's element. In it he was playing Hansen's game.

He worked left until he could see the stream, then
pushed ahead, knowing that for Hansen, too, the undergrowth dictated limits of visibility. The thought came and
went quickly, because he refused to dwell on it: that his
discovery of Hansen would be marked by the numbing
impact of a bullet. The pain would come later, only if he
survived long enough for his senses to howl in reaction.

He went on, pursued by his own breathing. Terraces.
The word began to repeat itself on his mind like the
repetitious chant of the Cuban sugar workers, pushing
themselves on with the words "la Caña" intoned hypnoti-
cally until they exerted themselves without thought. Then
the short synapse jump to Elise, her crazy Cubanized
English, the twisted syntax of her last words. He rearranged them until he had tried them in every possible
sequence, and still they withheld the precise admission

which would have convinced him. *Las terrazas.* The terraces. Hansen had to be waiting there.

But Hansen wasn't waiting there. A half hour later,
Locken scrambled on all fours onto the first narrow terrace, looking quickly around him, pistol ready.

Below and to his right the valley narrowed—the hour-
glass constriction that indicated the beginning of the pass
leading to Cudwyp. Below to his left were Miller, Femi,
and Mack, in that order, the older man close to the girl,
as they waded along the stream still fifty yards short of
the entrance to the pass. He could have shot them with his
pistol.

He looked up, saw the brush across the valley stir. A
second later the massive shape of Moses Nyoka rose into
view. Locken could see the look of puzzlement on the
stern black face. He shook his head, and got a corre-
sponding shake in return.

He moved off along the terrace several hundred yards.
He could look the entire length of the pass. Once the
others entered it the chance of ambush was nil. The
nearly vertical rock walls were scored clean of vegetation,
the pass looking as though it were gouged from the earth,
a gray, loam-colored scar that had never healed. In
places the stream had undercut the bluffs so that the walls
overhung the narrow path, providing protection from
above. Here and there, without support, the bluffs had
sheared off, leaving the path and stream bed strewn with
broken rock and small boulders. Ample cover if they
needed it.

One man could have held the pass with no hope of
surprise. Held them, hoping the others armed with Stens
arrived before the sound of firing was recognized in
Cudwyp, and police sent to investigate. Once they were in
the pass Locken could defend in both directions until help

arrived. A standoff, which for Hansen meant Nyoka's safety, and eventual loss. A thought began picking at Locken's brain.

Still unbelieving, he went along the terrace until he could make out the top of the Ferris wheel a half mile away, marking Cudwyp. Then he returned quickly to where he had seen Nyoka.

The others were passing below him now, invisible for the moment, sheltered by trees overgrowing the stream.

How many other choices did Hansen have? Ambush had been the most logical. As had the terraces. Hansen had chosen neither. Even Nyoka had recognized in an instant that the chance of finding Hansen, had he decided to lie in wait, was slim, until he fired his first shot. But Hansen had been given nothing to shoot at. In his searching, Nyoka's concealment in the thick brush had deprived him of a target.

What then? Hansen could do nothing but wait. Wait until Mack and Femi and Miller moved past, knowing that at some point Nyoka would join them. Wait quietly until a clumsy Locken went by, saving his bullet for his ultimate prey. Then take them from behind.

Locken's eyes shot rapidly back over the route the others had followed. They stopped, fixed on a point several hundred yards distant, where the overhanging gallery of trees thinned, leaving windows in the vegetation, a dozen feet square. His eyes jerked from one window to the next then back again, for a moment unsure.

He brought the radio up. "Mack."

"Roger." The signal was thin.

"You into the pass?"

"Almost."

"Take cover and stay there. Hansen's behind you, coming like sixty."

22

LOCKEN FOUND the boulder several feet from the point where he intersected the path.

He had descended almost vertically from the terrace. Down the valley side, brush tearing his face, his left knee rigid in protest as his heels dug into moist earth.

He dropped swiftly behind the boulder. At that point the valley narrowed, the valley floor no more than fifty feet wide. The stream flowed a few yards to Locken's left, the brush thickening to his right. His eyes followed the path in the direction Hansen must come. He had only seconds.

His line of sight for perhaps twenty yards was unobstructed, strangled at a single point fifteen feet away by an odd configuration of undergrowth. He was in position behind the boulder when Hansen came into view; the automatic was in Locken's left hand, cradled firmly in the palm of his right, the canted surface of the boulder serving as a makeshift bench-rest.

Hansen moved toward him in an easy trot, running slightly stooped. The heavy double-barreled rifle swung almost like a pendulum in his right hand. Fast, but too careless.

At the range of forty feet Locken sighted, adjusting for the rise and fall of Hansen's left thigh. If he had to shoot he judged his bullet would strike slightly above the left knee.

The call to Hansen was on his lips, when the dark shape slid abruptly into the corner of his vision. Moses Nyoka burst from brush not ten feet to Locken's right, stopping bolt upright in surprise.

"Get back!"

Locken shouted without turning, seeing Hansen react instinctively to the movement, the muzzle of his heavy rifle swinging up in a smooth half-circle. Locken shot quickly, unwilling to chance it. Hansen's gait took an awkward hop. He pitched forward, firing from the waist as he fell.

The cavernous roar of Hansen's rifle and the thunk of the heavy bullet came as one sound. The trunk of a small tree disintegrated two feet from Locken's left shoulder, showering him with jagged splinters.

Hansen dropped behind the oddly shaped configuration of brush. Locken studied it with growing suspicion, picked a point, and fired. His bullet whined off harmlessly. Beneath the brush was an outcropping of solid rock. Locken swore and looked to his right.

Nyoka had reacted quickly. His massive bulk seemed to have narrowed itself behind the trunk of a pale birch tree, his face turned toward Locken expectantly.

Locken motioned him to stay flat. Nyoka shook his head and made a snaking gesture with his huge hand, fingers extended. He was going to try to circle Hansen. Locken shook his head violently, but Nyoka turned away. Locken started to yell but changed his mind. Not until he was sure.

"Is that you, Locken?"

The sharp voice from behind the rock outcropping, coming down hard on the "k" in his name. The Afrikaansaccented English, different than Locken remembered, but unmistakably Hansen.

"It's me, Rickard."

"A good shot, Locken. The scar I'll have to remember you."

"I'm two ahead. I hope you're not bleeding to death."

He heard a hard laugh. "I'll live a long time, my friend."

"Just long enough will do."

"We will work together sometime, perhaps. You are a smart man, Locken."

"Smart enough to doubt that, Rickard." Locken looked past Hansen's hiding place. The path was empty. To right and left, nothing. "Where are your friends?"

"There is no one. Just me. But you should have escaped while you had the chance. That wasn't so smart."

"Not without saying good-bye." Locken squinted in thought. "Toss out the cannon, Rickard, and we'll talk."

"After you, my friend. You'd kill me I think."

Locken cocked his head slightly, listening. The sound of Hansen's voice had shifted a few feet to the right.

The safest way for Nyoka to circle Hansen would have been along the stream bed, using the bank for cover. To do so meant Nyoka would have to move from his original position behind the birch tree, past Locken, and another few yards to the stream. It would have taken time. He had chosen instead to go right, deeper into the brush. The narrowness of the valley floor, Locken knew, prevented too wide a swing; at some point Nyoka would have to pass almost under Hansen's nose, and if Hansen kept moving right, it would be more dangerous still.

Armed with the shotgun, Locken guessed, Nyoka would try to close to fifteen or twenty feet at the least. A bullet from Hansen's rifle could slice through undergrowth every inch of that distance and still make a mess. Nyoka must know that. Locken swore under his breath in frustration.

He considered a call of warning. He knew it wouldn't prevent the stubborn old man from whatever he intended to try; but it would spoil any chance he might have of surprising Hansen. If the choice came between risking the two, it would have to be Hansen. The decision made Locken smile; it had been easier than he thought.

He mentally ran through the precise sequence of events necessary if, to support Nyoka's move, he had to make a rush. Rise without sound. A half-dozen strides to cover fifteen feet. Over the rock outcropping. To find Hansen exactly where? the rifle aimed in which direction?

His eyes searched where Nyoka had to be and saw only dense brush, unmoving.

"You're very quiet, my friend. Planning nothing reckless I hope?"

"I wouldn't kill you, Rickard. Not before I learned a thing or two."

"You'd like to hear about that night, yes?"

Locken frowned at the tone in Hansen's voice. An anxiousness. As though it were as important for him to tell it, as it was for Locken to know.

"That's it, Rickard. Nothing in return."

"You will give me what I want, Locken. You will see. But I will give you something gratis. You were set up, my friend. Wrodny was as good as dead from the minute he entered that farmhouse."

"If that was free, how much do I get for a dollar?" He felt perspiration begin to form, cold on his forehead.

"You must have thought about it over and over, Locken. How did this Rickard Hansen fool me?"

He heard Hansen stifle a grunt of pain. Still farther to

the right, narrowing the corridor Nyoka must use to circle him.

"You were inside waiting. There was no other way."

"Hah." The rustle of leaves, again the grunt of pain. "You would have had to be a carpenter and a plumber to find me, Locken. An old house, yes, with many places to hide. I could have waited a hundred places, and still I think you wouldn't have found me. Behind a wall, with the plumbing, in the room to wash clothing. I came in the wall from the top, through the floor boards from the floor above. Down the piping like a fireman. Then I wait. Just me and the rats and the spiders, without moving when they walk across me. For six hours, Locken. Before I came out for Wrodny. No eating." He laughed. "No nothing." The explanation had tumbled out compulsively.

"You must love your work, Rickard."

"Like waiting for a leopard. Only a leopard is more difficult."

"Who wanted him? The Chinese? The Russians?"

"One of your own firms, Locken."

The question came angrily. "Why?"

Hansen's laugh was careless. "I had not the slightest interest."

"Only in the money?"

"Oh, no." Hansen chuckled. "It's the game. Like Houdini, eh? Under the ice, the risk self-imposed. The ultimate test, my friend. Make the game difficult, and the victory becomes worth something. With Wrodny it was the self-discipline of the wait. And that you were the best. About Wrodny himself, I knew only he was to die before morning."

Those months ago, staring at the ceiling from a hospital bed, Locken had reasoned that much and one step further. The morning before he was to fly out, Wrodny was to have spent with two MI5 interrogators from London, part of the arrangement for their letting him come across to the Americans in England, without making a stink. Locken had guessed that Wrodny was killed to prevent his talking to MI5. What he might have told them he would never know. Maybe Wrodny himself hadn't known. Mention of a name. An odd fact. And some carefully architectured deception would have blown away like a column of ashes. Locken hadn't cared.

"Who bought the contract, Rickard?"

"The big question, I think. If you guessed I was inside before you came, then you know. I'm not a mind reader, my friend."

"I want to hear it from you."

"Cap Collis. Does the sound of it make you feel better?"

There was no feeling at all. No anger. No release. Nothing. Not even surprise. Only a doubt that wouldn't go away.

From the point of Hansen inside the farmhouse, before the arrival of Wrodny, before they had set up the elaborate warning systems, Locken had drawn a line toward Cap Collis. Collis had found the farmhouse, and had been the only person who knew about Wrodny with enough warning to have staked out Hansen beforehand. Locken had been unable to make the final connection. The reason why: SYOPS's brief had always been protection, pure and simple. Assassination was CIA business.

"Collis had no reason."

"Collis had a very good reason, my friend. If I hadn't been . . . troubled by the Wrodny business, I wouldn't have cared to find out. But when Elise Roqué mentioned Collis I asked her many questions."

Locken moved forward on his elbows. "Elise knew Collis? Knew his name, you mean."

"More than his name I think. Well enough to know he once ran a network of agents in Cuba for the CIA, from a lawyer's office in Key West."

"How would Elise know that?"

Hansen laughed. "Because she was one of them. Collis recruited her after her disillusionment with the revolution. Disillusionment. A word for our time, yes?" Hansen's sharp laughter came back at him from the valley walls, mixing with his own. To Nyoka they must have sounded like madmen. "You think it's funny, my friend?"

Locken had a vivid memory of the Isle of Pines presidio, of Elise Roqué pointing an accusing finger while Raúl Castro watched him with those unfathomable oriental eyes.

"An old joke about a leopard that changes its spots, only not soon enough."

"They never let go of her, I think. It was the same with Collis. With your SYOPS he occasionally could have been quite useful."

"More than useful, Rickard," he said almost inaudibly. At some point SYOPS came in contact with most political defectors and agents on the run out of Eastern Europe. In the eyes of the intelligence establishment, some of them, like Wrodny evidently, were potentially more dangerous than desirable. A Collis strategically placed and willing to wield the scalpel in a little quick preventive surgery was worth whatever they had done to secure his position.

"So Collis said kill Wrodny, only you went him one better." Locken felt his throat tighten. "Why was I the lucky one?"

"Unpleasant for us both, I'm afraid."

"I'd like to see the smile on your face, Hansen."

"Oh yes . . ." Hansen's voice hushed abruptly, as though something else had drawn his attention. Locken heard the finely-machined rifle breech open and close as Hansen replaced the expended cartridge. "I regret that night very much, Locken."

"How's that?"

"That I didn't make a good job of killing you while I had the chance."

"You might learn to live with it."

"Enough already, I think." Hansen's voice was strained. "I would have killed you that night without a thought. Quickly and cleanly, as Wrodny and the young one died. It's the way a creature should die, Locken."

Hansen's confession was flowing freely now, Locken pushing it on as much for Nyoka's sake as his own. If Nyoka was within range, he had chosen not yet to move.

"Why didn't you?"

"Terms of the contract, my friend."

It took Locken a moment to fully understand. "You mean Collis told you to shoot me like that?"

"In exact detail. Why one man would want another wounded in that manner, I can't understand. Envy. Perhaps jealousy. Only words to me. The exact reasons you know, I do not. I think our friend Collis is a bit bent, yes? He became excited when he described how I should shoot you. Like a man readying himself for a woman." Hansen gave a cruel laugh. "Only I think maybe a woman wouldn't give him such pleasure." His voice dropped slightly in pitch. "Not a woman, I think."

"Recognize the symptoms, Rickard?"

The laughter this time was somehow forced. "Perhaps, my friend. But I'm sure Collis and I seek different pleasures. Wounding sickens me. The third shot I couldn't do.

It is no way to leave a man." Hansen's voice trailed off, as if his head had turned as he spoke.

"It won't buy you a ticket home," Locken said, then added quickly, "Throw the gun out, Rickard. Before it's too late."

"I don't think so," Hansen replied slowly. "Where is Nyoka?"

Locken felt his stomach knot, knowing suddenly it could all go wrong. He moved up on his knees, readying himself.

"I hear you move, Locken. Don't play the tricks with me."

"No tricks, Rickard."

"Tricks amuse me, Locken, but at this moment unwise. You see my finger is on the trigger, a very sensitive trigger. And my weapon is pointing toward a great dark creature I've watched stalk me through the brush. Were I to laugh, my weapon would surely go off and the creature . . ."

"Don't bluff now, Rickard."

"Bluff?"

The deafening roar of Hansen's rifle ripped the silence beneath the trees, a dull echo rolling away along the valley.

"Moses!"

Nyoka's voice came weakly from thirty feet beyond and to the right of Hansen's hiding place. "Intact, Mr. Locken. But a bullet came very close."

"As close as I intended, my friends."

"I must be old indeed. I've m de a poor job of it."

"Not so poor," said Hansen. "Only not so good. I've another bullet, Locken, you understand?"

"I understand."

"I want your pistol. Throw it over to me."

Locken tossed it over the outcropping without hesitation.

"And now Mr. Nyoka should stand very slowly. Without his weapon. So I can see him better."

"Mr. Locken?"

The point had come. Locken nodded, knowing there wasn't a choice.

Nyoka rose from the undergrowth. He stood helpless, waiting, hands at his sides.

Hansen suddenly leaned over the outcropping toward Locken, his face ashen. "Now you. Stand, please." The heavy rifle followed Locken to his feet.

"You're not going to shoot him, are you, Rickard?"

Hansen smiled, his forehead wrinkling. "Not after I've done so much to keep him alive."

23

"You've known long, my friend?"

Hansen spoke at him sidewise, the heavy rifle aimed again at Nyoka. The old man had taken several hesitant steps forward, his bewilderment lasting a little too long measured against the quick reaction to stress Locken knew him capable of.

Then he understood. Hansen hadn't had time to reload. His rifle held one bullet, yet the separation of Locken and Nyoka meant a swing of the barrel ninety degrees between them. Beneath the incredulous look on the old man's face was a calculation Locken recognized. Across Nyoka's back, held in place by his braces, Locken could see the tip of the brush knife.

"I've known about ten seconds. When your first shot didn't kill him."

"So, you know something, too, about Rickard Hansen, I think."

"When we made it to the pass and you hadn't tried to stop us, I began to wonder why."

"Pass." His forehead ridged slightly.

Locken nodded toward the rifle and saw Nyoka take a step forward as Hansen looked up at him. "You've won the game, Rickard. You don't need that."

Hansen put some effort into a smile, his eyes sliding

quickly around. "Were you to kill me now, my victory would be less than complete, yes? This protects me against my friends as well as enemies." He swayed as he spoke, as though leaning into a wind.

Locken could see where he'd shot him. A nickel-sized entrance wound in the meaty part of the left thigh. Little bleeding. No exit wound.

Locken kept digging, the gaps of doubt still yawning at him. "You took a big risk at the apartment house, Rickard."

"By necessity, my friend."

"He nearly had us all, you mean." Nyoka's tone was still unbelieving.

Hansen's head went toward him. "Locken knows better, I think. What was I to do? The setting obviously required my talents. Had you walked from the door of the apartment house I would have had to invent a reason to miss." He looked back at Locken. "You didn't give me the chance, fortunately. I was pleased to see you, but Bouche's insistence on the help of outsiders made our little game more difficult, eh?" He started to smile but his lips went pale.

"The gunmen in the alley, Rickard. The one that came out from behind the green gate."

Hansen's forehead rose in question. "You couldn't have seen."

"Seen you shoot him?" Locken shook his head. "But when I shot he smacked into the taxi, instead of going with the impact of my bullet. It happened too fast to think about then, and the next minute you were there on the fire escape."

"We must have shot at nearly the same time. A magnum bullet gives the bigger push, eh?"

"It was a big chance."

Hansen considered the words almost with pleasure. "The bomb in the taxi was the bigger one, I think. The bomb frightened me very much."

"Bomb?" said Nyoka, taking a step closer. But he overplayed his incredulity.

Hansen pivoted awkwardly, bringing the rifle to his shoulder with a quick snap. "No, no, my friend." He smiled with a touch of arrogance. "It would be a pity to spoil it now. Move again and I'll kill you." There was a suspended moment when Nyoka looked as if he would accept the challenge. "Tell him, Locken."

Locken hesitated, then nodded. "He'd do it, Moses. It's not worth the chance."

Nyoka paused, then took a step back. Hansen lowered the rifle. "Really, gentlemen. You owe me these few moments. If Bouche had been successful, you would never have left Heathrow. He was quite mad, and equally determined. One goes well with the other, yes?"

"Determined enough not to make a stupid mistake like hooking the cord of the auto bomb over the frame of the taxi." Locken added with measured question in his voice, "Or hiding the beeper under the front seat."

Hansen laughed quietly. "Bouche put it on top of the petrol tank. Under the seat I knew it would be discovered. I thought it would be destroyed." His voice carried a slight pique.

"You could have destroyed the contraption yourself," Nyoka countered, still reluctant.

"And fertilized an already growing suspicion. After the apartment house Bouche began to watch me strangely. An absence of both an explosion and a radio signal would have been too much, I think." He spoke to Locken with thin admiration. "But you did not destroy it, my friend. You were as determined as Bouche."

"I thought Elise had done it for some good reason. The taxi was parked close to the staff building. The stewardess uniform would have given her access."

"As did the simple expedient of workmen's clothing. You believed what you wanted to, my friend. Elise was a dangerous, unpredictable young lady."

Nyoka's expression thawed, breaking in to a narrow smile. "How well I nearly found out."

"You warned us with the taxi horn, at the Angel?" Locken found himself wanting to know.

Hansen made a small, stiff bow. "A feeble effort, but all I could think of. It worked, yes?"

"It worked," Locken replied slowly. "What was supposed to happen?"

"At the inn? No clear plan, except to sugar your petrol and delay you. Bouche and the driver went to that strange village to phone London. He would have had a hundred men by choice. Quite mad. Elise found the uniform on a clothes line and it gave her the idea. She dressed herself as a charwoman and walked straight in the front door. I could do nothing but wait in the dark and watch a thug try a thug's trick. I was prepared to kill him myself. Instead I watched you." He smiled, a thin white line of mouth. "Very skillful."

"You went to great efforts to keep me alive," said Nyoka.

Hansen spoke quickly. "Wrong, my friend. To prevent the others from making a successful kill. A fine distinction, but for me an important one." He gained strength as he spoke. "I play this game for myself, no one else. I create the risks, so that they might be overcome." He laughed scornfully. "There is no pleasure in certain victory, my friend, and this time winning meant making others fail. An interesting variation, I thought." His shoulders went slack. "You mean absolutely nothing to me."

Nyoka's gaze fixed on Hansen curiously. Locken sensed it too. An integrity of a sort, perverse, arrogant, but firm in its governing of Hansen's actions.

"Weren't the odds against the three of you tough enough, Rickard?"

"Odds?" He lowered the rifle a few inches and stared at Locken, uncomprehending. "There were no odds. Not one chance. Drawing out the elements against Aman to crush before they became powerful, the assassination of our friend here, all as carefully engineered as a moon trip."

"Nonsense," said Nyoka sharply. His head strained toward Hansen. "My scurrilous brother-in-law could have sent killers any time in the past three years. I'm not really that important."

Hansen grinned and shrugged. "Someone convinced him you were. Your dying here would serve more interests than Aman's."

"The idea wasn't his?" Nyoka's eyes burned into Hansen.

He brought the rifle up in reaction, and spoke to Locken almost apologetically. "Elise told me who was behind the plan to kill Nyoka. The all-powerful." His voice had contempt. "The thought of going against them appealed to me."

"Elise was a plant with Aman."

"They don't let go willingly, do they Locken? At the end Elise had nothing of herself left."

"Was Bouche with them too?"

"No." Hansen paused thoughtfully. "Bouche needed only his hatred. For nationalists of any kind, preferably off-white. Nyoka might have been Nyerere or Kaunda, or

Boumédienne. The names mattered little. In his mind
Bouche was still fighting the F.L.N."

"You should have killed him while there was just the
two of you," Nyoka said, cold with rage.

"Not easily done. The driver watched me carefully.
Bouche made a special arrangement with him, I think. I
never had the chance." The sadness was exaggerated.
"Colleagues should have more trust."

"And now you came back to tell us about it." Locken's
thoughts jumped ahead from fact to fact, trying to make
the final connection that would mean complete understanding.

Hansen's eyes met his. "About the shooting. I wanted
you to know." A harsh rattle of pain convulsed Hansen's
entire body. He lowered the rifle, resting its tip on the
rock outcropping and looked away, the color draining
from his face. An odd expression bent his mouth.

Locken had the unreasoned impression that Hansen
was trying to find words that would bring some forgive-
ness.

He turned painfully toward Locken and slowly extended his hand. "No hard feelings, my friend?" He took
a single hesitant step around the rock outcropping.

Locken saw Hansen's face change to surprise the instant before the explosion blurred the high forehead in a
rising whirlwind of dust.

Two spikes of pressure drove into Locken's ears, as the
focused charge of tiny pellets enveloped the lower half of
Hansen's body, sweeping his legs from under him as
though snapped away by dragline.

24

WHEN LOCKEN looked again Hansen lay on his back, the angularity gone from his limbs. The lower half of his body was dappled scarlet. Locken reached him in quick strides.

"Good God," said Nyoka, bent over them, his face chalk-gray. "What happened?"

"Someone left the autobomb rigged where that outcropping narrowed the path. Hansen tripped the cord when he stepped toward me."

"But who?"

"It had to be Mack or Miller," Locken said, seeing the surprise give way to thought in Nyoka's expression.

He turned to look again at Hansen. Behind the shock-glaze in Hansen's eyes, Locken could see panic. "Locken . . . make it a clean kill." The words came separately.

Hansen's arms stretched awkwardly toward the double-barreled rifle; the fingers reaching short, clawed at the earth pitifully.

Nyoka's face contorted. "Let him have it. He's a dead man already."

Locken bent his face toward Hansen. "Why the plane, Rickard? Why shoot down the plane?"

Nyoka's eyes pinched with question. Hansen stared up at Locken without understanding, before his head moved loosely from side to side. "Saw plane after . . . Nearly met you along stream. Had to hide."

Locken's thoughts reached back to the hollow sound of stone against stone he'd heard as he waded toward Evans's farm after the plane had been destroyed. There wasn't time for Hansen to have downed the aircraft, return unseen to the clearing where they'd left Burt, then work back to the longhouse and pasture via the stream. No time and no reason.

That left only one person in position to put a bullet into the pilot of the aircraft. Even as the word "Miller" formed on his lips the facts tied themselves together with agonizing clarity. Collis's connections with the CIA, and their intention to have Nyoka murdered in Britain. His manipulation of Locken's own blind need to confront Hansen. And the final, sickening understanding of why Cap Collis had insisted upon Miller.

Nyoka moved at his side, Locken sensing his thoughts had run parallel with his own. Locken reached out, but already the gigantic black man had turned, drawing the long brush knife from across his back. "He has my girl, Locken."

"If he gets the chance, he'll kill you. That's why he's here."

"My girl," Nyoka repeated, and started to move. Locken lunged for him, but the old man sidestepped agilely, swinging a clubbing forearm. Locken spun sidewise, caught his balance, but Nyoka was already running back along the path in the direction of the pass.

Locken yelled at him. The old man didn't turn.

He drew out the radio and thumbed the transmit-button, the pounding beginning in the back of his throat. Mack's acknowledgment was feeble beyond the diminishing strength of the signal.

"We're on our way. Watch Miller."

"Sorry, Michael." The reply came back emptied of tone. "Jerome is being his usual pain in the ass."

"Watch him, Mack!"

"I did my best."

The sound of Miller's carbine reached Locken on two vectors. The first shot reverberated toward him from the direction of the pass, echoed with tinny accuracy by the radio in his hand. Locken stared at the radio gone suddenly dead, unwilling to comprehend. A second shot followed the first, separated by a brief, sickening interval. Locken flung the radio away.

"Locken . . ." Hansen's voice was a plea now.

Locken snatched his pistol from the ground, the advantages and risks of taking Hansen's rifle balanced mentally in a split second. He'd have needed two good arms and then some.

"Locken . . ."

Locken stopped long enough to push the heavy rifle toward Hansen's outstretched hand. He saw the high forehead relax, the pink slash of a mouth trying to grin. Then he began to run.

His eyes were already set on the path ahead, aware of nothing but his own strained breathing, when from behind him came the thunderous report of the heavy rifle, a single, final shot.

Locken found Mack a few feet beyond the narrow entrance to the pass, where the dense brush of the valley thinned, and finally disappeared completely.

He lay on his face, a single bullet hole squarely in the center of his back, a second six inches above it.

Locken turned away and began running again. Ahead with a hundred-yard lead, Locken caught a glimpse of Moses Nyoka.

His strides were graceful and smooth, his gait powerful,

varying slightly in adjustment to the unevenness of the path. The brush knife was in his hand, swinging rhythmically with the pumping of the black man's thick arms.

Locken called him again, yelling to stop, to wait. His shout was unheeded.

Locken ran after him, knowing that it was a run of no other creature on earth, a broken restricted lope, the right leg continually ahead of the left. At some lower level of consciousness he was aware of the workings of his knee, a parting of cartilage and tissue. But still he ran, watching in helplessness as Nyoka's strides drew him farther ahead.

Nyoka's lead was still lengthening when he came to an abrupt stop. At a point where the path reset itself in a slight angle to the left, Locken saw the reason why. Fifty yards beyond Nyoka, Miller waited calmly in the exact center of the path, the girl next to him. The trench coat had been pulled off her shoulders down to her waist and tied in place with the belt, pinioning her arms around behind her back, stretching her pale blouse tight across her breasts.

Nyoka watched, frozen. Locken saw Miller's face lighten with a grin. He reached out toward the girl, his eyes fixed on the old man.

Locken knew what was coming. "Moses, no!" he shouted, as Miller caught the front of Femi's blouse and tore it away, taking the brassiere with it. In the charged stillness the sound of tearing cloth had an ominous clarity. Nyoka wavered as though losing his balance. Then Miller's hands began moving over the girl's body, kneading her great dark breasts, an adolescent fondling without feeling, his head turned, watching Nyoka's reaction.

Femi tried to step away, but Miller drew her to him, the girl's struggle only making him more calculating in his job of torment.

Locken could almost hear something snap. Before

Locken could reach him, Nyoka lunged forward with an angry, hurt bellow. His heavy shoulders bunched around his thick neck. Locken could hear the grunt breathing now, the hoarse intake of oxygen of an animal near its absolute physical limits.

Miller moved clear of the girl, no longer having use for her. Femi tried to step forward, to put herself between Miller's carbine and her father. Miller used the weapon to backhand her across the head, stepping past her while she was still falling. He waited, grinning, watching Nyoka striding toward him, no more than forty yards remaining between them.

Locken stepped quickly sidewise, raising the pistol, knowing that at greater than a hundred-yard-range it was absolutely futile. Approaching Miller, Nyoka's gigantic frame blocked out all beyond it.

He braced the pistol in both hands, breathed, and squeezed, firing past Nyoka in the vain hope of hitting Miller. He saw the bullet strike the rock wall, short and to Miller's left. He fired again, mentally ticking off the shots. One into Hansen's thigh, another ricocheted from the out-cropping.

Two wasted now at Miller from too great a range. Four left, eight in the clip in his breast pocket.

Again he began to run.

Already Miller had dropped to one knee, bringing the carbine up to his shoulder, the grin clearly visible, then hidden suddenly, as his cheek hugged the stock of his weapon.

Locken felt the last bits of conscious control leave him as Nyoka, unvarying in his pace, bore down on Miller.

At a range of less than twenty yards Miller fired. Locken heard the shot-slap of the heavy bullet strike Nyoka. His great body reared up, faltered, then bent again, plunging on.

Locken fired on the run, seeing the bullets strike the rock walls around Miller without pattern. Undistracted, Miller raised the barrel of the carbine slightly, and fired at Nyoka again, trying for a head shot.

Running, torso thrust forward, Nyoka had wrapped his arm across the front of his head like a crown. Locken saw Miller's second bullet lift the arm from his head in impact, spinning Nyoka to his left.

He smashed like a drunken man into the rock wall, turned, caught himself, and went ahead.

Miller stood up, the grin gone, the girlish mouth twisted in panic. Nyoka was within twenty feet of him, stumbling, weaving, the long knife raised, when Miller fired. Two shots close enough together to sound as one report. Nyoka took them, tripped on nothing, and fell forward motionless.

Miller looked up, seeking Locken. The grin spread again. He walked, almost a strut, toward Nyoka's fallen body, measuring the distance Locken had to come, confident of time. He slipped the bullets into his carbine one at a time and stepped over Nyoka.

Running, Locken hammered the final clip into the automatic and fired from chest high. Miller jumped sidewise in surprise, a wild lucky shot, close, but not close enough. Miller leapt forward over Nyoka's body, in a quick dive for cover.

Locken ran twenty feet farther than he should have, a sprint to bring him within effective range. Knowing that Miller would step from cover, carbine up. About now.

Locken went for earth, the vacuum-suck of Miller's bullet inches from his right ear.

Prone, gun extended and cradled, he made a slim target. Miller was no target at all. He had moved a yard sidewise, the carbine sighting at Locken between two jagged rocks. Locken fired at the gun barrel, and saw

Miller withdraw it quickly. His only hope was to fire each time Miller leveled the carbine to try to damage the weapon. It was a tactic good for exactly five remaining bullets. Locken forced himself to concentrate again on the join between the two rocks, not sure at first why his eyes had been distracted.

Then both eyes shifted not more than a few degrees, focusing suddenly in range beyond Miller.

Moses Nyoka's left arm had reached out from his body, like the leg of a crab. It felt earth with a flattened palm.

The arm straightened, pushing the massive torso up. Knees still touching, thighs like pilings driven in the ground. The great head lifted. Then the bloodied chest. Finally the right arm, the long knife still clutched in a knotted fist.

Nyoka stood, his eyes rolling upward, around, and down to where Locken knew was the huddled figure of Miller. A turn of Miller's head, and Nyoka would never realize the purpose that had willed his body from the ground.

Locken was on his feet without thought or expectation. Miller saw him rise, and stood in disbelief, the grin spreading across his face as he leveled the carbine.

Locken shot then, flinging the pistol aside when it no longer responded, urging his body to cover the few score feet that remained between them.

Miller fired only once, with great care.

Locken felt his left knee explode, the sensation pulled from a past nightmare. The clear remembrance of pain to follow wrenched a yell from his lips.

He went down fighting the wash of unconsciousness sweeping up from below, knowing that Miller's next shots would move carefully along his body until, bored of playing, the finisher would pierce his brain.

His head bent up, trying to loose words as his final weapon of defiance, hearing a saw-edged "sonuvabitch, sonuvabitch" crackle from his own throat.

He thought he saw Miller turn away, Nyoka over him like a breaking wave, arm upraised. A quick, sickle-flash of reflecting light, Miller's grin lifting on a gout of crimson, the carbine dropping away, no longer held close to the small body. A nerveless crumpling, sliding away from beneath the grin now warping on a bloodied face.

Then the hotness pulled Locken down into it. A great roar of sound chased him deeper, a single word, catching him and expanding until it filled his entire brain, Moses Nyoka's cry, *"fisi!"*

25

COFFIN SMELL, musty and dead.

A cocoon of pain held him. Locken opened his eyes, stared at the gray mist above, and fell back into the swirl.

Later he tried again, unsure of how much time had passed. The mist became a ceiling. His body was damp and hot beneath a rough blanket.

Locken breathed stale air, and recognized the thick walls of the longhouse, turning his head against neck muscles rigid as steel. Femi bent toward him from a chair a few feet away, Hansen's double-barreled rifle across her lap.

His mouth tried some words, and Femi blurred in his vision. He tried again and heard a ragged imitation of human speech saying, "I'm sorry."

Then she was at the window, carrying the rifle. "I buried him, Locken. In an unshaded place, the way they do at home. I'll come back sometime, if I can."

He ran his tongue over cracked lips. "The others?"

"Left for the carrion eaters. Miller's soul will rot with his body, I swear." Her voice lost the bitterness. "There wasn't time for your friend."

"What time is it?"

Femi shrugged. "Before noon. I don't know."

"Who brought me here?"

"I did. Carried you partly. You were in and out."

Her right cheek had an angry red mark across it, her ear was caked with dried blood. She nodded toward the strip of pale blouse tied around his knee. "The brace stopped most of the bullet, but you need a doctor."

In place of the blouse she had fashioned the mauve scarf into a makeshift halter for herself. Locken was surprised in a dull way how well it suited her. He pulled the blanket back and forced his legs over the edge of the bed, biting off the flash of pain that ran up his body. "I'll take that."

She gave him the rifle. "I waited but no one came."

Locken snapped it open, ejected the expended cartridges and stared at two empty chambers. "Let's hope nobody will."

He stood. The room tilted.

"Careful. What are we going to do?"

"Leave. The quickest way possible."

She glanced toward the wall, as if she could see through it the distance to the pass. "I can't go back there. Not yet."

"We'll try Evans's farm. He had a car." He reached out toward her. "I need a hand."

They left the longhouse, Femi carrying the canvas bag, blood-smeared now, in one hand, supporting Locken with the other. At the edge of the trees she used his knife to hack off a dead branch and quickly fashioned it into a short gnarled staff. Neither of them spoke until they came to the clearing where Burt stood, torn open and broken. She stared at the taxi, eyes reddening, but no tears came.

"Why, Locken?"

"You mean Miller?"

She shook her head violently. "Why all of it?"

Locken worked the explanation over in his mind, turning the pieces this way and that, trying to make something that would have meaning for the girl.

"I can guess part of it, but I don't pretend to understand it." He spoke, the phrases choppy, words on top of words in a stranger's voice. "A man or a committee of men convincing themselves that killing your father, here, now, was necessary. It was profitable, redressed a balance, or maybe just gave them one mental jump on whoever their bogey man was this year. Then they signed an operations memo with a tag 'Expedite Termination' and went home to their other world, the one they keep separate out there in Reston or Georgetown or Watergate East."

The girl was tight-lipped, silent next to him. He stopped, listening, thinking how unnatural a human voice sounded against the gentle rush of water off to their left.

He went on, almost as though he were speaking to himself. "And while the gentlemen sip away at their gin and tonics, a Collis or Miller down at the bottom of the pyramid makes it happen. Business as usual. Killing called a lot of other things, so the good men at the top can go home clean at the end of the day. The ones down at the bottom don't care what it's called or why. Because they like their work." He tried to smile at the girl but it wasn't in him. "I'll tell you one thing. The people at top and bottom need each other. Perfect symbiosis, Femi, emphasis on the perfect."

"Who was it, Locken?" Her voice was flat.

"Hansen thought the CIA sold the idea to Aman. Maybe they did. Your father being killed here is going to make things uncomfortable for the British in a dozen African countries. The U.S. of A. won't lose by it."

He looked ahead, forcing awareness back into his senses. If the men armed with Stens were still around they would have pushed this far at least. He hoped his instincts weren't deceiving him.

She followed his gaze along the tire track, her voice distant, almost lost. "This Collis knew they were going to kill him."

"If he ran part of their operations here, he knew. 'Operations in Sector' memos and all that. Probably not the details. Among the spooks you don't learn anything unless it's essential, and at that point Collis wasn't in on it. Not until he learned from a gentleman at MI5 he called Smith that one of those three would try to prevent it. For Smith's own reasons he wanted Cap's help to protect your father. When that happened I imagine there were some very anxious long distance telephone calls."

Her dark eyes became cool and looked away. "Do you think he knew it was Hansen?"

"He must have had a suspicion. With what he knew about Elise and could find out about Bouche, Hansen was a better bet, which would have thrilled Cap no end. He already had his axe sharpened for Hansen because he'd defaulted on a very important contract."

He heard his voice say "yours truly," the giddyness already pounding its way up into his head. Where the stream ran close to the path he left the girl and bent to splash his face with icy water. The swirl kept rising. He felt the girl's hands steady him.

He breathed deeply until he'd pushed the feeling down, the girl watching patiently before she asked: "Why would this Collis want to shoot you?"

Locken brushed the water from his face with a shirt sleeve. "Collis originally contracted Hansen to kill a certain Czech trade official before he could tell what he knew to the British. It was a hasty kill order, but an important one, and Collis didn't have many choices. Somebody was going to get killed if Wrodny was to die. You want to make an omelette, Cap would have said, you have to break eggs."

"But why you?"

"I happened to be the guy on the griddle. Maybe Collis arranged it that way." Locken's eyes narrowed and squinted away. "Collis didn't regret it. By his measure I was going soft. In other words, I was beginning to think about what I was doing, the people involved. In our business that wasn't healthy." He paused. "There was another reason."

"You don't have to tell me, Mike."

"I probably couldn't have, until I'd heard Hansen. He thought Collis hated my guts, and not so deep down either. His wanting to wound instead of kill me was reasoned by a sort of childish envy. I could see it then. Cap didn't have a friend in the world he hadn't bought one way or the other. Even his wife finally left him, and he once asked if she'd written me, as though in some twisted way he thought I had something to do with it. Cap was an ugly man, and it bothered him more than anyone suspected. I guess he saw in me someone who had things he didn't. By Collis's logic, putting me out of action but alive to think about it, evened us up for a lot of things." Locken shook his head.

"And still he sent you and your Mack to protect my father?"

"He must have danced on the ceiling when the idea came to him." Locken stopped and looked at the girl. "Femi, he sent a guy who couldn't run or shoot, who wanted Hansen so bad he wasn't thinking straight enough to care about your father. Add a stubborn Scotsman with too much pride to admit he was going blind. Together, little enough to prevent the real assassins from reaching your father. And there was always the wild chance Hansen and I might kill each other in the bargain. Collis couldn't lose."

"Then why . . . Miller?" Her mouth seemed almost reluctant to form the word.

"Insurance. To help things happen. If the assassins failed, the job was his."

Her voice trembled slightly in frustration. "But he killed to protect us. At my apartment. And again at the inn."

"No, Femi," he corrected softly. "At your place those gunmen didn't know Miller from Adam. They would have nailed him as happily as the rest of us. He was shooting in self defense."

"Is that why he shot the woman?"

"Elise? He killed her because he wasn't sure." He saw the question in her look. "Hansen mentioned something that didn't register until later, about Elise walking straight in the front door of the Angel. It was a very brassy, very smart play. Better than poking around windows in the dark. Dressed as she was, she might have fooled anyone not expecting trouble."

"But you were waiting."

"So was Miller. Watching the front door with a gun in his lap. Whatever Miller was, he wasn't a fool. He saw Elise come in and let himself look taken in, hoping she'd make a successful play. Except it wasn't that easy." Locken's eyes fixed on a point, ordering it in his mind. "Check the register, find keys, snoop a few rooms. Figure what to do if you weren't alone. It took time. When I walked into the inn after the fight in the parking lot, Miller was having fits. And second thoughts. When he ran up the stairs and saw Elise, key in the door and no one shooting, he thought she might have been the double after all, there to warn us, maybe even join our team. He put a bullet in her rather than take the chance."

"He shot the pilot too?" Her tone signaled near-refusal to comprehend.

"His story about seeing something flash in the sun was a lot of cock."

"Don't, Mike," she said, reacting to his anger.

"He knew I couldn't take a chance that Hansen or one of them was out there, close enough to get a shot at the plane when it came. He shot the pilot, the sound of his carbine covered by the engine noise. Then he shot a bush a couple of times and ran telling us he'd seen Hansen."

"I believed him," she said quietly. "But why did Collis send the plane at all, if he wanted my father killed?"

Locken replied without hesitation: "Because I bullied him into it. When I talked with him on the phone he thought I'd try something rash if I didn't get what I wanted. Try something and probably land the lot of us in jail. If that had happened all of his intrigues would have collapsed. He had no choice but to promise the plane."

"Couldn't he have promised it, then done nothing?"

"Cap wouldn't risk that. In the event Mack or I survived and came back to point a finger. He'd protect himself. From the way he talked about his contact at Whitehall I think he probably picked the person he thought was most likely to bungle it on their end. If he failed, Cap was blameless. Anyway, he had Miller."

"But the airplane came?"

Locken thought of the pilot, the single brief glimpse of the jowly gray face, the walrus moustache. "Whoever Collis contacted was a better man than he figured."

She looked ahead again, her eyebrows pinched together until there was a tiny furrow between them. "I knew something was going to happen when the three of us were waiting. You and my father were hunting Hansen. Then the shooting started and Miller became very nervous."

"He'd left a surprise package behind and didn't know who'd open it."

"I don't understand."

"Miller rigged the cord of the autobomb across a narrow part of the path. He knew he'd catch someone. He hoped it would be your father or me."

"The bomb that was beneath the car?" Her mouth turned down in disgust.

"He must have slipped it into his gun case in the taxi. I don't know when he had time to place it with you and Mack."

"I know." Her face changed as though she'd tasted something sour. "Just before we came to the pass, Miller said he had to go off into the bushes for a minute." She looked at Locken, the same cool rage he had seen in her father's eyes lying below the surface. "He asked me if I wanted to come hold his hand."

"Go on, Femi," Locken said, pushing her past too much reflection.

"Nothing more. When he caught up with us he had that horrible grin again." She shook her head in revulsion.

Locken stopped, faced her, then asked it: "What happened with Mack?"

She shook her head fiercely, as if she were trying to loosen an answer from the things she was trying to forget. "I saw it, Locken. But I don't understand it." The hurt was in her voice.

Locken waited.

She began slowly. "When you called on the radio, after the explosion, Miller suddenly pointed the gun and told us to go along through the pass."

"He knew your father and I were alive, and somebody else wasn't. It meant it was up to him."

She shook her head again, bewildered. "But your Mack ignored him. He smiled and turned his back, like Miller wasn't there. As if Miller were nothing. Then he began talking to you on the radio."

She hesitated only a moment, aware of the pressure of Locken's hand on her shoulder, then went on.

"When he did it, Miller went crazy. He shot . . . he shot very close and very quick in the back." She stopped. "I can see your face. I think it's enough."

"It's enough."

26

THEY STOPPED where the tire track met the dirt road. Across the wooden bridge, the Humber sedan was alone in the farmyard.

"They're gone," Locken said flatly.

"You knew?"

"Hansen knew."

"Why would they leave?"

"They might have found Bouche's body and figured they'd never see pay day. Maybe Hansen sent them packing before he came for us. I don't think he realized there was a pass out of the valley." Locken made an angry move of his shoulders and stepped from cover.

He waited for Femi to catch up with him. Crossing the wooden bridge she asked: "Why did Hansen do it?"

Locken smiled faintly. "For himself. Something about self-imposed risks."

"Don't you understand?"

He glanced around at her. "A little too well. Push the risk out toward the limits. Win, and you feel closer to the gods than you think anyone ever has. The oldest game of one."

"And Hansen was like that?"

"Some people find out the only time they're alive is when they're laying it on the line. Hansen was like that."

He smiled at her, at the intensity with which she was trying to understand something completely alien.

Locken went on: "The trouble is you keep pushing that line farther out. To test yourself, you say. But down deep you know it's the only way you can keep getting that good, good feeling. Hansen pitting himself against Elise and Bouche, and maybe in his mind the whole CIA, was a risk right out close to the limit."

"And he lost."

"At least he found out where the limit was. Hansen was his own man, Femi, with his own set of rules. The odd thing is I understood him more than I'll ever understand the Millers of this earth. They're the new breed."

Femi bent her head curiously. "Perhaps because you and Hansen were the same."

Locken thought about it. "I hope not, Femi."

Her mouth tightened. "If only there hadn't been Miller."

"Don't start that," he said roughly. "Try to account for all the ifs in your life, you'll end up in a cage. There *was* Miller."

"Where would this Collis find a creature like that?"

The smile came and went quickly. "I think Miller was Cap's boy in more ways than one."

Femi frowned, then comprehension spread. "You mean they were lovers?"

"Stranger people have found each other in this world. I'd worked with Cap for years, Femi, and I'd never heard him say a soft word about anyone, male or female. Until he talked about Miller. When he did, something was in Cap's voice I'd never heard there before."

"Collis should be made to pay for this."

Locken shook his head. "There isn't a visible connection between him and your father's death. He made sure."

"What will he do when he finds out Miller died too?"

"I don't know. But I think inside, Cap's old nasty heart is going to break and then some."

Femi looked up at him, her face without softness. "I hope it kills him."

The keys to Evans's Humber hung next to several others on a wooden pegboard behind the back door to the utility barn. He had Femi stand well clear of the car until he'd gone over it as completely as he could without tools. The car had been untampered with; no other surprises left behind.

"I don't drive," said the girl. "But I'll try."

"With a little moral support I think I'll manage."

They drove east toward London, slowing occasionally when the wave of numbness reached Locken's head, washing yellow everything around him.

He stopped once, long enough to call the police from a roadside pay phone. When the voice at the other end lost a little of its reserve and asked him to repeat what he had just told them, Locken hung up.

At 1:00 P.M. the BBC reported the full story of the collapse of what Reuters had already labeled the abortive attempt to depose Aman. They listened on the car radio, Femi's fingers white against the door handle. Fourteen of the uprising's leaders had been tried that morning on a sandy beach in front of the entire population of the capital city, then shot by a firing squad.

Locken turned off the radio. It was a long time before Femi spoke: "It was over before he died." She shook her head. "Useless." She repeated the word several times until her jaw hardened around it.

"Your father knew it was too soon."

"The whole nasty, horrible thing—for nothing."

"You're alive." The girl turned quickly, the rage flaring. "I mean you've got a life in front of you to use any way you see fit. Your father thought that was enough of a reason to die."

She was silent until she directed him to turn onto the Ring Road, still west of London. The late autumn sun slanted behind them. "This will do."

"It may have to." Locken pulled over and stopped, the nausea trying to move up inside him.

Femi said, "I'm going back to Buwanda, you know."

"I was feeling the vibrations."

"I guess I knew it last night. Looking at those faces in Cudwyp made me realize what a stranger I am here. I always will be." She looked at him, the defiance gone, her face softened. "Buwanda doesn't need me, Locken. I need Buwanda. I think you must sometimes run from the things you need most. That's what I meant when I said I was afraid. There are things, people; and once you begin with them, you know you're going to lose yourself in the bargain. There isn't going to be any more you, all separate. You're going to be part of it or them, and you'll never be able to go back. It's frightening."

Locken took a long breath, the sweat cold on his neck, and nodded her to go on.

"I don't know what's involved, or how long it will take, but I'm going back. We're going to organize. Down deep I'm one hell of a political animal, I know it."

"Maybe it's the breeding, girl."

She smiled. "That's what my father kept saying."

"He had his way."

"He got to you, too, didn't he, Locken?"

"Yes, he did." Locken grinned, surprised at his own admission.

Femi sighed. "Now I'm going someplace quiet to think

myself together for twenty-four hours. Then I'll catch a plane."

Locken prodded his pockets, reached into one, and took out a crumpled wad of bills. "Soggy but spendable. Compliments of the U.S. of A. A contribution to the new party, whatever you decide to call it."

"Something appropriate, count on that." The slenderest hint of irony made Locken look again at the set of her mouth. She dug a small purse from the green bag on the seat between them, and stuffed the bills into it.

She opened the door and stepped out, then leaned back in. "Good-bye, Locken."

"You forgot this." He lifted the canvas bag, feeling the weight, and looked into it.

When he looked up she was smiling at him. "Do something with it, will you? I have what I need. You see, that's another thing I discovered. I'm not quite the sophisticated city lady I thought I was." She smiled again, a sure, strong grin. "There's a lot of Africa in me, Locken."

She turned quickly and walked toward the taxi rank, pulling the trench coat more tightly around her. An icy wind had blown the sky clear, and Locken realized he was cold.

27

"YOU'RE ONE sad-looking fucker."
Locken bent close to the mirror and studied his eyes.

That the face was his he couldn't deny. But the eyes.
Rings of putty-gray around dilated pupils, his eyelids
swollen.

He leaned away from the mirror and finished tying the
black silk bow tie a second time. He hadn't used it enough
to crease the material along well-worn lines. The knot
drooped.

He took a step back and glanced over the three-year-old
Austin Reed tuxedo, bought when he was eight pounds
heavier, and worn exactly as many times as the tie. It
didn't fit well. A wire coat hanger had left a sharp inden-
tation across the trouser legs halfway down.

He shrugged, brushed the lint off the shoulders, and
drained the bourbon from the glass balanced on the wash
bowl.

He poured it half full again on his way through the
kitchen, dragging his leg behind him, stiffened and en-
larged at the knee by six yards of Ace bandage, and
deadened by two carefully injected ampoules of Novocain. In the bedroom he took the small suitcase from the
closet and lifted it onto the bed. He rummaged out three
feet of stranded No. 10 wire with small alligator clips on

either end. A nine-inch jimmy, a roll of Scotch dialectrical tape, a dozen or so copper nails, and a small screwdriver with an insulated handle. Not exactly the tools of his trade, but essential when he had dealt with alarm systems.

He considered taking the small Browning automatic but left it. The knife would be enough.

Back in the kitchen he stuffed the wire and tools into Femi Nyoka's green bag, which now bulged conspicuously, but he couldn't help it. He drained his glass, placed it in the sink, and went to have a last look of assessment in the mirror.

"Good evening, Mr. Ambassador, Mr. Vice President." He grinned at the face in the mirror. "Sorry. Other way round." Then the grin was gone. "Not such a smart fucker either."

He looked at his watch, found its hands hadn't moved since the last time he looked, hesitated, and went to the phone. He dialed a familiar number and asked for Liz.

"Mike? Your voice . . ."

He cleared his throat. "I said, I want you, Liz."

"You're drunk."

"Bed. Sunsets. Peace."

"Don't talk nonsense, darling, I'm about to go on."

"Finished, Liz. Retiring."

"I don't believe you." He could hear the caution in her voice. "You *are* all right?"

"Alive, alive-o. Only one more thing to do."

"Mike, no."

"Have to, Liz. Then I'm coming for you. Be ready, or I'll tear the place apart."

"No, darling." He waited out the longest pause of his life, before he heard Liz's wonderful husky voice saying, "Me. Tear *me* apart."

He slipped on a lightweight plastic raincoat that would fit later into his pocket, and took five minutes to go down three flights of stairs.

He caught a taxi easily. It was a half hour before the-aters in the West End emptied; a steady stream of yellow "For Hire" signs moved east. Three hours before, he had parked Evans's Humber in a carpark near Norland Square and walked away from it. He'd spent the time since going over it in his mind, working on his knee. When he'd done all he could he floated his senses upward again with bour-bon and a fifteen-grain Dexamyl spansule, watching the clock as he drank. He didn't want to peak out too soon.

He told the cab driver Regents Park Zoo, ignoring the look that went casually from face, to cheap raincoat, to green canvas bag. A hand reached out and punched the meter with some reluctance.

Locken scarcely noticed. He was already reviewing the security arrangements in effect at the Ambassador's resi-dence for a reception honoring the Vice President of the United States.

First, the Metropolitan Police. At least a half dozen, with reserves close by in case of trouble. All uniformed, positioned at carefully chosen but unobtrusive points along the block on either side of the Ambassador's sprawl-ing, gaudy, Edwardian mansion near Regents Park. Painted and plastered gaudier still by a team of Holly-wood set designers flown in because the Ambassador had been unable to find anyone in England with the right flair. The press had treated the Ambassador in kind. A very big house, thought Locken. And the police all outside.

The dangers were inside; at least he knew the drill. Two Marine noncoms on the outer gate, two more at the front entrance, with loaded side arms. Tough combat veterans, career types, their duties thankfully narrow in both scope and locale.

A Marine officer acting as duty officer on the telephones, and hovering behind him a waspish FSO-2 named Weaver slotted as a cultural attaché, serving as Embassy chief of protocol. Among his least enviable tasks, the job of discreetly interrupting conversations to page parties for incoming calls. Then there was SYOPS, drafted for the occasion, inside, with the guests, probably the full London contingent of six. Plus Cap Collis.

The Vice President's Secret Service battery was another eight, all especially trained. P.P.D.'s. Quick-reacting, hardened professionals, who wavered continually between paranoia over an unanticipated handshake and deadpan matter-of-factness about the bullet-stopping contingency they all willingly accepted. Locken had never met one he would enjoy drinking with; but he respected them.

Locken paid off the taxi, stepped from it carefully, and walked toward the zoo. It was closed.

When the taxi was out of sight he turned, crossed the narrow park bordering the street, and followed the trail running parallel to Regents Park Canal. He looked at his watch.

Exactly thirty-seven minutes later, according to the brass ship's clock on the Ambassador's mahogany desk, he was alone inside the ground-floor library. Raincoat in his pocket, he might be mistaken for a guest who had lost his way. Until someone looked in his canvas bag.

The library was a showpiece. Cream-colored walls and gold trim, hardwood floors, high brocade draped windows facing southeast across Regents Park. Locken stepped to the double door opposite the windows, opened them less than an inch, and listened. Beyond the door a wide hallway led to the front of the house then made a right-angle turn toward the west wing and the reception. He could hear music, a trio playing "Hello, Dolly" with a pronounced rock beat. The Ambassador liked to be thought of as "with it."

He closed the doors and went directly to the desk. He pressed the red button on the fluorescent desk lamp, and craned back the oblong hood, until light spread over the entire surface. It had a top of red inlaid leather.

It took him not quite two minutes. The trio was playing music from *Hair* when he discarded Femi's bag, picked up the phone, and punched the last button in the series of four. He dialed the number beneath the first button, waited, then saw it light.

He heard a crisp hello in a manner he recognized, if not the voice.

He gave the single-word access code that would signify the call was official security business and held his breath.

"That word is no longer operational, sir."

"Look, I'm in the library. On button four. I have to talk with my boss out of the mob. I missed the briefing, is all." No bullying, a slight touch of frustrated helplessness.

"It's Marathon. Get the dope on the rest of the Man's week from your number one, O.K.?" Adding as an afterthought, a barely scornful, "sir."

"Right. Let me talk to Collis. And thanks."

Locken heard the Marine call Weaver.

"Hey wait . . ."

"Sir?"

"Just tell him Mr. Miller is waiting in the library."

"That all?"

"That's all."

Locken put down the receiver. He walked to the double doors and pressed his ear against the crack between them.

A moment later he heard the brittle click of Cap Collis's Florsheim brogues on the serpentined marble floor of the hallway, coming briskly in the direction of the library. He was whistling "Yankee Doodle" in rhythm with his step.

Locken moved away from the doors, walking quickly to the high window that led to the rose garden. He bent toward the jumper wire he had used to bridge the alarm system, and grasped one of the alligator clips gently.

A slight pressure of thumb and forefinger and he could predict the next 30 seconds with absolute certainty.

Cap Collis would open the door to the library at almost the exact instant a pair of warning lights blinked red at two Secret Service agents watching the alarm system control panel in the bowels of the house.

In less than three seconds the Motorola pocket pagers in a dozen tuxedo jackets would beep the exact number of times to start hearts thumping through a maximum security alert. Cap Collis would be no more than a half-dozen steps into the library when all hell would break loose around the Vice President. In less than thirty seconds four more Secret Service agents would arrive at the point the alarm circuit had been ruptured, weapons out, ready to shoot. Finding no reason to shoot they would demand in no uncertain terms an explanation for what they had found. What they would receive was the question. At that moment Cap Collis's thoughts had best be in tight order.

Locken plucked loose the jumper wire and stopped only long enough to glance one more time at the desk.

In its direct center, the boyish features highlighted by the desk lamp, Miller's severed head, carried in Femi's bag, grinned at him, the whitened lips pulled back over the grainy teeth, in angry rictus.

"Hope he'll recognize you without your glasses, Jerome."

Locken stepped from the library, went across the rose garden, along the precise route he had come. At Regents Park Road he waved down a taxi.

He climbed in and sat for a moment, drained of feeling, of pain, even sadness.

The driver slid back the window between seats, waiting. Locken stared at the unfamiliar face, wondering vaguely if he ever thought about symbolic gestures.

Locken spoke finally. "There's a club in Mayfair. Near Sybilla's, just off Berkeley Square." He smiled at the driver and knew it was a senseless smile.

"You all right, guv?"

"I'm fine."

The driver was still looking at him when Locken leaned back and shut his eyes.